Aoife's Bible

a historical novel

by

Blaine Turner

illustrated by

Olivia Wiering

Surely there is no more wretched sight than the human body unloved and uncared for... Oh, this was the great ploy of Satan in that kingdom of his: to display such blatant evil one could almost believe one's own secret sin didn't matter... In order to realize the worth of the anchor we need to feel the stress of the storm... No pit is so deep that God is not deeper still.
                              Corrie ten Boom, 1971

Remember that if thou hadst more faith, thou wouldst be as happy in the furnace, as on the mountain of enjoyment. Thou wouldst be as glad in famine, as in plenty.   Charles Spurgeon, 1858

If damnation be justice, then mercy may choose its own object.   Jonathan Edwards, ~1740

L'audace, l'audace, toujours l'audace.
                   Georges Jacques Danton, 1792

The original texts of the modern hymn
"Be Thou My Vision" are in Old Irish.
English translation by Mary Byrne, 1905
Irish Bible quotes: William Bedell, 1685

Hymns in the New World are from Isaac Watts, 1674-1748. Quotations of the fictional Finny Haddon *in italics* are from Charles Spurgeon, 1834-1892.

Au Clair de la Lune, Un Canadien Errant, and *À la Claire Fontaine* are traditional folk songs which can be heard on the internet.

Telugu on page 155 is by Joseph Janga. The drawing of Bridget was inspired by a photograph of Zia Miller, age 10, and Bridget's little story was written by Mackenzie Ulfurts, age 7, both used by permission.
Bridget's prayer at the end of the book is adapted from old Puritan prayers.

Aoife's Bible

Text copyright © 2017 by Blaine Turner
Illustrations copyright © 2017 by Olivia Wiering

ISBN: 978-0-578-19909-2

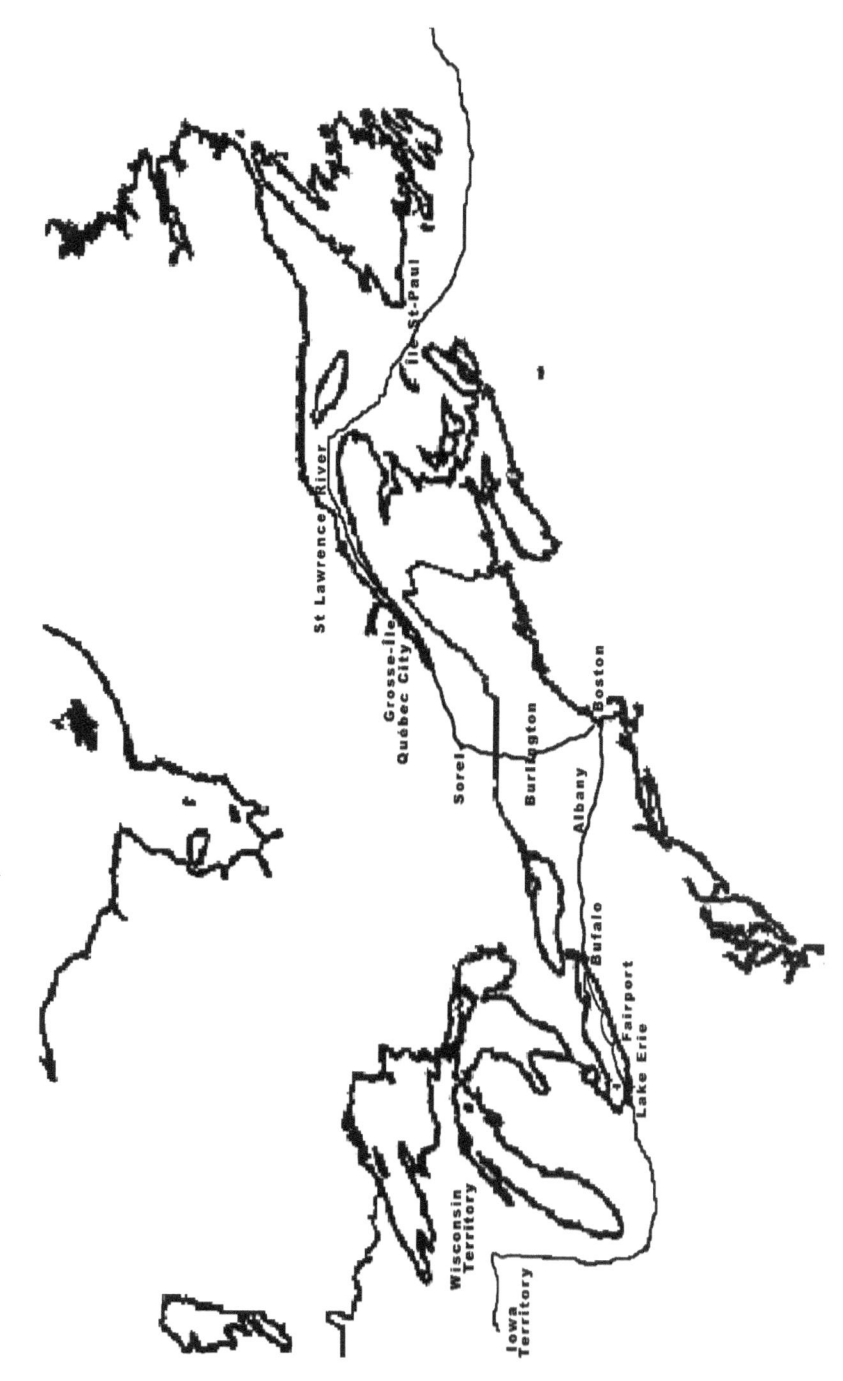

St Lawrence River

Île-st-Paul

Grosse-Île
Québec City

Sorel

Burlington

Albany

Boston

Bufalo

Fairport

Lake Erie

Wisconsin
Territory

Iowa
Territory

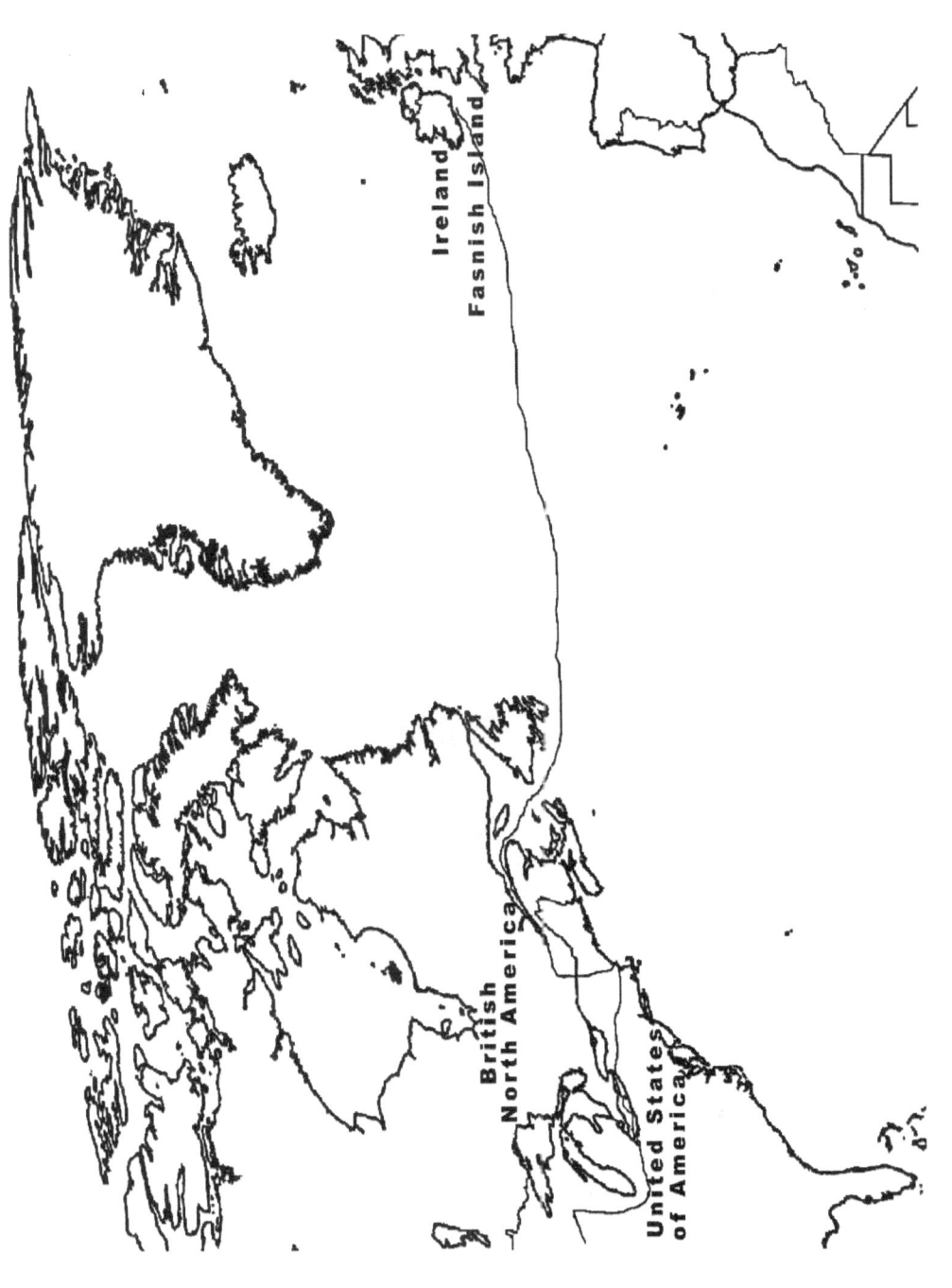

Honi soit qui mal y pense.
King Edward III, 1348
May he be shamed who thinks evil of it.
Hear tell of the gutter but keep your mind out of it.

Bridget

Chapter 1

Rop tú mo baile, a Choimdiu cride:
ní ní nech aile acht Rí secht nime.
Rop tú mo scrútain i l-ló 's i n-aidche;
rop tú ad-chëar im chotlud caidche.

Be thou my vision O Lord of my heart
None other is aught but
the King of the seven heavens.
Be thou my meditation by day and night.
May it be thou that I behold even in my sleep.

The Cottage

How dead must you be before you can find new life?

This is a modern legend of Aoife (pronounced EE-fa), which means "beauty." The year is 1847, along a rugged seacoast in your mind—reminiscent of Ireland just before the Ballycotton lighthouse was built. In the old legend, set in the time of Christ, the girl was a warrior princess, defeated in single combat by a demi-god hero he-man jerk trained by her sister. Then they became lovers. She was a buff, buxom beauty with a huge spear and enough blood-red hair to blind any sized man. The real drama queen of her era; now she is buried and forgotten. But some ancient things should never have been forgotten. Indeed, we ignore some deep-rooted writings at our peril.

For we are not fighting against flesh-and-blood enemies, but against evil rulers and authorities of the unseen world, against mighty powers in this dark world, and against evil spirits in the heavenly places. Ephesians 6:12

On the other hand, the more recent Aoife O'Day was young, gaunt and weak. Yet unforgettable. Her arms and legs were but sticks jutting from peasant clothes. Her fiery red hair was unruly and shedding in places. Her big eyes, set wide but sunk deep into a pale face, danced cordially but inhabited a limp body and languid soul.

I'm writing this as her devoted sister, now at the end of our journey together. This is her story, a tall tale perhaps, yet bear in mind it's we Irish we're dealing with. Where tall becomes true.

Back then hers was known as the most haunting face around Blarnybrae—because you can never quite take all the allure out of a goddess. There's something elusive that keeps drawing you in, as to a sweet, but fatal Siren song. Every morning before the cold fog lifted she'd rise from a thin pile of straw in the corner to stoke the small fireplace. She used peat bricks she'd sliced from an ancient bog the previous week. Like her Lord, they were about 2000 years old. They served to fend off the chill and damp before the others got up. As thick grey smoke climbed the wall up to the chimney pipe, she'd sit and gently stroke the protruding ribs of Dog Angus. She could lay her bony fingers between them. He lived on what rats he could catch, which was a much better diet than the thin potato gruel she'd boil up later.

But God was new every morning. This was the only time of the day she could steal for Bible reading.

I mo chroí d'fholaigh mé do bhriathra, ionas nach bpeacóinn i d'aghaidh.

The old words of her language were sweet as sunrise over sea, and fresh every dawn.

I have hidden your word in my heart, that I might not sin against you.
Psalm 119:11

But sin was indeed stirring in the dank air as she huddled in her blanket. She had just come of age, complete with skin blemishes and new embarrassing feelings swirling inside. She tried to damp them down, as she would the fire, but they kept smouldering. Sinful, surprising feelings in a body so shapeless and ugly, she reflected. Moods inappropriate for a starving, motherless child.

She had killed her own mother in childbirth and the father had abandoned her for a whiskey bottle and a three-master to America. What little money they had, went with him. Rumour had it he died of typhus and was thrown into Boston Harbour. The money went to the deckhand who stole his shoes.

Aoife and her siblings were parcelled out among different, distant relatives in far-flung villages. Some died of starvation, others were said to have been taken by wolves. Impossible? Not in this bygone land. In time, she lost track of all of them. Now she lived in a place that exists only in wild nightmares.

The fire at her white knees went out so she puffed at it with thin, trembling lips. Ever so gently, then more forcefully until she became faint as the flame grew strong. So frail and hungry she was, like the thin, flickering tongue near her mouth. It began with a cord of thick, grey smoke climbing up her hair to rise again toward the mud brick chimney in the wall. Its pungent smell was deceitfully comforting in her nostrils, like the potato water would later be in her belly. As the flame grew, her cheeks took on its colour. Gently she hung the black cooking pot above the fire and stirred it with a long wooden spoon. In the dim light the utensil appeared as an extension of her bony arm.

The girl's adoptive family were cottiers, farming a plot of stony ground bequeathed by a faraway king to his foreign lackeys as payback for favours. This king had conquered her country decades before and now had bled it almost dry. Most of the crops were sent overseas as rent to wealthy landowners, forcing Aoife's new family to glean a meagre existence from the dregs. They worked three acres of potatoes, set out in the spring and harvested in the fall when the stalks died. Some were kept to plant the next spring. They also had a cow, two pigs and twelve scrawny chickens. There were extra taxes to be paid for owning each animal. At least they could get eggs and milk and use the animal manure to fertilize the crop. Occasionally Aoife was sent out at daybreak to collect seaweed at low tide. She had to get there before the other farmers got all of it. Traipsing back, she had the long strands draped over her like a bridal gown. She would then spread them ceremoniously over the potatoes. Now a terrible blight was spoiling what little food was left—a tiny morsel of which was beginning to heat under her careful eyes. The animals had to be sold to pay taxes. The land was suffering horribly from rape. The people as well. It was like a monster ravaging her mind.

Entranced, she was sitting in the loose straw by the fire when the others arose. Bridget came first to nest in her lap and help turn the thin, frayed pages of her Bible. She was a pixie with deep blue eyes and a button nose. Dainty wings on her narrow shoulders would not have seemed out of place. Her wild, auburn elflocks smelled of peat smoke and her only garment was a crude burlap smock, which fit like a tent. Her face looked prematurely wise, her countenance infectiously sad. Still her little-girl purrings were soothing as the two huddled together against the cold. Aoife's heart beat faintly against her pink, pointy ear as they stroked each other gently.

Aoife continued reading softly in Psalm 119:

> *19 I am only a foreigner in the land.*
> *   Don't hide your commands from me!*
> *20 I am always overwhelmed*
> *   with a desire for your regulations.*
> *21 You rebuke the arrogant;*
> *   those who wander from your commands are*
> *   cursed.*
> *22 Don't let them scorn and insult me,*
> *   for I have obeyed your laws.*
> *23 Even princes sit and speak against me,*
> *   but I will meditate on your decrees.*

Bridget seemed asleep, probably just faint from hunger, but asked weakly. "Effey, whose commands are we supposed to obey? Daddy's? The mean landlord's?"

"We obey all commands," Aoife said, "except when they go against God's laws."

"But where do we find these laws?"

"Right here in our Bible, Biddy," replied Aoife, giving her a squeeze. "Will you help me find them?"

"Sure." The little wisp sat up a bit and a thin hand reached out to finger the page edges.

"Jesus, Mary and Joseph!" The father burst into the room. "Yous always got time for that feckin' book when there's work to be done outside. And fetch some fish from town today."

"Can I have a few coins then?" Aoife murmured.

"Shut your gob," the father said. His voice came from the gut which overhung his rope belt. "I've no coins here. Get'm the way ya doo before."

"I try, Dadaí." She closed the Bible, leaned toward Bridget's ear, and whispered, "We'll start tomorrow." Aoife placed the limp girl gently in the straw and stirred the simmering broth again. She had taken to giving the child part of her own meagre portions. The father and brother always ate the most because they had the hardest work, or so they said. Still, it was the mother who was up just after Aoife, tending to outside chores. And it would be the

12

mother who would be sweeping the stone floor after all the others were asleep.

"Well, are ya gunna fiddle with that pot all day?"

"No, I amn't, Dadaí." Fearing a beating, Aoife got up to leave. "Can I take Biddy with—to help carry?"

The father just turned and retreated into the bedroom and his whiskey bottles. The bottles contained much more than gruffness. Aoife had a name for each: pride, envy, anger, sloth, greed, gluttony, and lust. She was beginning to wonder from which ones she herself might be already sipping.

2nd Chronicles 7:14 slipped into her mind.

"Then if my people who are called by my name will humble themselves and pray and seek my face and turn from their wicked ways, I will hear from heaven and will forgive their sins and restore their land."

The Sin

A vast ocean away, and several years earlier, a young man named Jean Marie Delacroix (žawn ma REE DEL a kwa) knelt at an ornate altar in the Cathedral-Basilica of Notre-Dame de Québec. Like the building, he was well appointed with fine features and fancy clothes. He had black hair and deep blue eyes. His straight nose, small red lips, and waistcoat made him resemble a grasshopper. This

13

garment had whalebone stiffeners and was laced tight in the back with reinforced buttons up the front to mould his waist into a fashionable silhouette. His arms and fingers were long and delicate, his ears cocked back like a cat. He wore a red boutonnière in the lapel of his frock coat. Most people thought of him as nothing but a boastful cockalorum. But at the moment he was begging forgiveness for sin. Like Aoife, he had his Bible tucked under one arm. And like her, it was well-worn in the language learned at mother's knee. However, it was not the Irish translation by William Bedell, but the French by Antoine Genoud.

PSAUME XXXVI.
8. Réprimez votre colère et contenez votre indignation, de peur que vous ne soyez ému jusqu'à faire le mal. 9. Un jour les méchants seront exterminés; mais ceux qui attendent le Seigneur posséderont la terre en héritage.

PSALM 36.
8. Repress your anger and hold your indignation, lest ye be moved to do evil. 9. One day the wicked will be exterminated; but those who wait on the Lord shall possess the land by inheritance.

Jean Marie's hands were folded until the knuckles shone white. His head was bowed over the communion rail and he was mumbling something to the red carpet below. "Was I so wicked as to be disowned and thrown out of my house? God! So what if I was admiring a flower you put along my backyard path one night? Her petals enticed me, her stem drew me. I was simply enjoying my hand close to her blossom to shelter it from the breeze. I

14

tingled when it drew close to emit its fragrance. Such be your purpose and the value of scent. I was being sweet and tender, just wanting to admire rose petals in your good hand. Therein my sin—with the garden plant you gave me. Call it a mistake. Cut flowers. Mistake yes, and then murder when she wilted and died, leaving me alone with the issue. Because she was an Irish rose, our little bud is in Saint Bridget's Home on McMahon Street. You know the place. Because I am French, I'm entering your little seminary here. Take me; rape me; slay me; I hope you get more satisfaction than I did."

Chapter 2

Rop tú mo labra, rop tú mo thuicsiu;
rop tussu dam-sa, rob misse duit-siu.
Rop tussu m'athair, rob mé do mac-su;
rop tussu lem-sa, rob misse lat-su.

Be thou my speech, be thou my understanding.
Be thou with me, be I with thee
Be thou my father, be I thy son.
Mayst thou be mine, may I be thine.

Blarnybrae

The way to Blarnybrae town wound down alongside Bungosteen Creek with clear water spilling white over random grey stones. It was paved with crushed slate, glimmering like ice in the new morning light. Fragile rays filtered through the old, knotty trees of Muckanagheder Woods. Branches angled off trunks like lanky arms and sparse leaves became skin, hair and warts. Gnarls appeared as prying eyes. Roots developed feet and toes. All was a misty dampness with lush green moss growing on everything. The two wee girls huddled together as they plodded along safe under a

shared blanket. If something should grab them at least they'd have each other.

"Be ye scared?" Bridget asked in a thin voice. "I can feel a Pooka in here."

Because she was from a different part of the country, Aoife asked what she thought a Pooka was.

"Oh it's a horrible deformed goblin," Bridget whispered ominously. "It inhabits dank shadows and snatches kids for supper. It has warts, a long nose, slit eyes, and a pointy grey beard. Its teeth are not fangs like a wolf, but flat, sharp chisels. People say it always carries a smelly o'possum on its shoulder."

"Oh Biddy," Aoife said, clutching her Bible. "We don't need to fear any such leprechauns or faeries. We have something stronger." She directed them to sit down on a nearby moss cushioned rock and pulled out the book. "Here it is, Isaiah 41:10. Can you read this Biddy?"

Ná bíodh eagla ort, óir táimse maille leat: ná bí lagbhríoch, óir is mise do Dhia: neartóidh mé thú, fós cuideoidh mé leat, coinneoidh mé fós suas thú le láimh dheis mo cheirt.

Don't be afraid, for I am with you.
 Don't be discouraged, for I am your God.
I will strengthen you and help you.
 I will hold you up with my victorious right hand.

"Effey, then why isn't God strengthening us right now? Why are we so poor and hungry? What does God have against two innocent farm girls?"

Aoife shrugged her shoulders and confessed she didn't really know. She always found it easier to love God more fully with a full belly.

Wearily they continued on, out of the forest, through the town and then onto the docks where the big ships moored. She was alone on her last trip here and had been able to distract a young fisherman with a smile. As she held his eyes, her hand had slipped some mackerel into a bag beneath her apron. Now she was glancing around but didn't see anyone familiar. What's more, her conscience was nagging again—about stealing. Clearly it was a sin, even in the grip of hunger pangs. Nevertheless, the plan today had Aoife flirting with men while Bridget ducked under their tables to help herself to whatever might be in the buckets. Even fish heads and guts would greatly improve the potato soup at home.

Suddenly there he was, a handsome prospect with broad shoulders, scruffy beard, and inviting blue eyes. He was alone, sorting fish at a massive wooden table. She approached hesitantly. "Are these for sale?" she asked grinning, "Did you really catch them yourself? My, how silvery they are in the sunshine." She blinked in amazement. "Are you the captain of the ship?" She looked up at him sideways and squinted as if the sun were in her eyes.

"I just sort the fish, ma'am." The boy seemed shy but plastered his attention on her friendly smile and sprigs of long red hair beckoning from beneath a scarf.

"Then perhaps could you just sort a tiny one into my wee bag here?" Aoife pulled at her smock just enough to reveal a little pouch. "I'd be ever so grateful."

The boy looked away. "They watch me like a hawk," he muttered. "There's lots of freeloaders around. Want something for nothing."

Aoife looked shocked. "Sir, do you take me for a beggar?"

"Oh no, not you," he said, probing her eyes.

Meanwhile little Bridget, crawling on the ground, had found no buckets underneath. So momentarily a thin arm reached up and yanked a small fish off the table. Catching this out of the corner of her eye, Aoife moved close into the young fisherman, indicating he should slide a fish under her apron. To her surprise, he did just that and started reaching for another. Their hips touched.

"Bejeezus Faolan, what's the story with the lady?" The bellowing voice came from the wheelhouse of a fishing trawler—just as the hand beneath the table snatched another cod. "Wait right there, I'll be right down!"

Panicked, Aoife tried to move away but the sailor grabbed her arm. Simultaneously a tall, silver-haired figure appeared out of nowhere and started to lead her off by the shoulders. "Come Colleen girl," it said. "We must make for home before the gnomes overrun the trail." He brushed the fisherman's arm aside with his shillelagh (shuh-LEY-lee) and gripped the back of her garment insistently. Bridget scooted behind them and followed down a narrow alleyway.

The man hobbled along surprisingly fast on his gnarled and crooked cane. He had smeared lard on carved blackthorn, then shoved it up a chimney until it cured a nice shiny black. The knobby head he'd filled with lead to make a formidable club.

20

The Cellar

After several turns on the cobblestones, they happened upon a tiny door that led down some narrow steps into a dingy basement.

"We'll be safe here," the old man muttered, his gaze constantly shifting.

"But who are you?" Aoife demanded, her eyes darting toward the door.

"You'll not be wanting the police here, will you?" he said.

Bridget stood petrified.

"My name is Lenna Ó Leannáin," he said, tipping his Paddy cap, "I'm pleased to be your rescuer. You must lay low here till the coast be clear. Let me have those fish so's the smell don't give us away. Might yous be hungry?"

"We're always hungry," Bridget turned brave; her name means "strong." Then her breath caught in her throat as she noticed the man's face in the thin light beam from above the door. He had a skinny, wrinkly nose, slit eyes, and a long grey beard. It looked like he was wearing a rosary as a necklace. She glanced over at Aoife, but her sister seemed unperturbed.

"What are you going to do with us, Mister Lemon?" Bridget asked.

"Oh Alanna, my child," the man said, "First I must recite to you the poem I'm writing. I have no choice. Just one stanza for now. Then I'm going to go fry up these fish so's you can have a proper dinner.

Poem Love

1
Before the texts of all the books,
Before our history,

Before the tales where legends grew,
A timeless truth there be.
It's not a creature, not a wind,
Nor gem of any kind.
It's no mere diamond cut from rock—
This Spirit Song we find.
One word's enough for our poor ears,
One drop to quench our thirst.
But now He speaks a waterfall,
Until our hearts should burst.
We're plunged in shining pools headfirst,
In realms we can't recall.

"Colleen girl, you'll watch over little Alanna, won't you? Be silent as lambs, they're looking for yous. They're not nice people." With that he swept through the door and locked it loudly behind him.

"Effey, what is this place?" Bridget asked. "I didn't understand the poem."

"I think it's some kind of cellar for storing potatoes, or whiskey or something," Aoife said.

"Or little girls," said Bridget, "did you see the man's nose and beard? I think he's a Pooka for sure. I saw a tail under his cloak."

"Oh Biddy, don't be silly. A big nose and beard doesn't make someone a boogeyman. He's trying to help us. Besides, where I come from some Pookas are nice. John 10:10 says, *'The thief's purpose is to steal and kill and destroy. My purpose is to give them a rich and satisfying life.'*"

Bridget pursed her lips. "But how do we know who is the thief and who is from God?"

Aoife looked at her blankly. The room was devoid of any furniture. And no windows. They decided to lie down on some hay in the corner. They huddled into their blanket and tried to nap, but slept only fitfully—each not wanting to wake the other.

"I could make better poems than him, anyway," Aoife said:

Is there a poem?
Then there must be a poet.
A creation? God.

It wasn't till late that evening the man, whatever he was, returned. A big key rattled loudly in the old door lock. He slipped in, carrying a wooden bucket. "Here's plenty of soda bread and hot fish for you." The girls just stared at him amazed. "What? Oh this? What's so strange about wee Scannalan here? He's a harmless fox-ape. And don't you think he blends in well with my beard?"

Harmless or not, riding on his shoulder was a good sized possum with scraggly grey fur, a creamy white face, and black eyes and ears. Its pointy snout did match the shape of the long beard into which it nestled.

Disturbing, but at least the pink nose seemed cutely inquisitive and Scannalan didn't seem to smell at all. The girls sat back against the wall and dove immediately into the bucket of food. It was more than they usually had in a week. The bucket also contained a whiskey bottle full of creek water, hopefully filled upstream from the town.

While they were eating Lenna Ó Leannáin recited more of his poem:

2
We stand in lands without a world,
And marvel at His might.
Yet His soft hand is comforting,

And everything is light.
His beams shine bright on three clear sides,
Burst forth in single one,
And pulsate hues of rhyme and note,
In concert never done.
We tremble in each other's arms,
Afraid to even cry;
What is His name, this awesome sun?
We'll learn it by and by;
We'll read it in the bluest sky;
We'll see it when He's done.

"Now the police are looking for yous, also the fishermen," Lemon wrinkled his forehead even more than normal. "I be thinking yous best stay put for the night. You're finding the straw soft enough, aren't you Alanna?"

"Thank you," Aoife said, "but why are you helping us?"

"Araagh! Colleen girl, dinna ya know pretty young girls are not safe in these parts? There's fairies about that will steal a child and leave a wee elf changeling in its place. Fairies are not the petit winged lasses depicted in pictures, but the dark, evil siths of reality. They have supernatural powers. And if a child droops and withers like poor Alanna here, she's fairie-struck for sure and a fairie physician must be summoned at once. She's wanted in Fairie-land as a bride for some prince, so they pine away mysteriously till they die. I happen to be a Practitioner Emeritus and I'll ask if we can hide yous in one of them big ships. Meanwhile keep this door locked." He vanished as abruptly as he had appeared.

"Big ships?" whimpered Bridget. The girls just stared at each other wide-eyed.

The fried fish soon disappeared and the soda bread after it. They washed it all down with the creek water, but milk from their cow would have been so much nicer. Only the cow was sold long ago.

After a nap they were thirsty again but the bottle was empty. "Effey, did you notice there's no loo in here?" Bridget was standing in a corner with her legs slightly crossed.

"All we have is the bucket," Aoife said helpfully. It seemed to fit the bill adequately.

The light was beginning to dim so Aoife reached for her Bible. She was used to reading by firelight so she turned easily to Isaiah 41:17-18. Bridget snuggled into her lap.

"When the poor and needy search for water
*   and there is none,*
*   and their tongues are parched from thirst,*
then I, the Lord, will answer them.
*   I, the God of Israel, will never abandon*
*   them.*
I will open up rivers for them on the high
*   plateaus.*
*   I will give them fountains of water in the*
*   valleys.*
I will fill the desert with pools of water.
*   Rivers fed by springs will flow across the*
*   parched ground.*

"That's very nice, much prettier than Lemon's poem," Bridget said, "but God is mean to just promise things and then not give them. I'm thirsty now."

Aoife frowned at her. "Biddy, you can't describe God based on what's happening now or even how you feel about him. God tells us who he is in this book. He promises us not just a drink of water, but rivers and fountains of it. Can you believe that?"

"Maybe someday if you help me," the little girl said.

"Maybe someday I'll really feel it myself," said Aoife.

With that, they nestled up together and a strange darkness descended upon them. It was more than just turning out the light in a bedroom. It's as if the walls begin slowly closing in upon you, and then just as you're about to be crushed, they move right through you and disappear into a deep cave of blackness. It lays over you, smothers your eyes and crushes your breath. It's a strangling reptile at your throat.

Words came to Aoife:

Cold, crushing stone walls,
Urine wafts with tortured cries—
Candle of hope dies.

The two girls were set adrift, huddling and spinning slowly in black space until up and down become meaningless, directions inappropriate, locations invalid. In the void of the room, they had only each other and their awful imaginations.

Light casts not shadows
In Christ, no darkness at all—
The shadow's from me.

Bridget was trembling, small and weak before the looming emptiness consuming them. She felt lost and alone and shivered like a kitten. Aoife tried

26

to engulf and protect her but she herself was too frail to defend against feelings of abandonment. The older girl felt left for dead and in desperate need of strong, caring arms about her own wilting shoulders. Bridget whimpered softly as an army of monsters approached and began sniffing at her body. One began licking her face. She couldn't see, but smelled its damp hair and foul breath. Her face became sticky with its tongue. She closed her eyes tightly and shuddered.

"Hush," whispered Aoife, putting a hand over her mouth and little nose, "there's evil men hunting us out. Ones that lurk in the shadows and drag girls in with them. We'll be safe if we're quiet as church mice." Aoife said this but she didn't believe it for an instant. She pictured torches, at first in the distance, then approaching. Dark figures circling— then pawing, clutching; rough hands dragging them apart. Then carrying them off separately, each to her own particular horror. "Poor Biddy," she imagined. "Take me but leave her be—the small and innocent one."

Execution hood—
Your death sword will turn on you.
Choose now life in Christ.

The darkness brought no real monsters or men, but instead other imagined molesters of the mind. One after another. The night became long. Bridget in desperation wriggled around and embraced Aoife as a sister—no, more than that. Her tears wet the breast nestled next to her as onto a mother. Aoife coddled the little one who became her own dear baby. She stroked and kissed her hair reassuringly.

They clung to each other seeking warmth—their backs against the air growing cold around them.

Nestled between them was the book they cherished. They could feel it pressing into their hearts. It was a ray of hope, but lost to them for want of light to read. Bridget pictured it as a magic book full of healing and miracles. Surely it would be comforting to think on this. The god of her gut would surely rescue them soon. He promised and she could rest in that. Still she was uneasy. Her heart was divided, waiting, wondering, then doubting. Would this god be pleased or even be able to help?

Aoife, for her part, was more confident in the power of the Bible, but maybe was she just using it as a talisman to act as a charm to deflect evil and bring good fortune? What she really wanted was a special girlfriend, not a book or this baby Bridget. A true soulmate would be something to hold on to, something to stand with her against evil men and the powers of darkness. But there was no girlfriend here, only the Bible. And the god of her gut was just that—only a friend. And where was this friend in the pit of her stomach, the rock bottom at road's end? It was beginning to look like the god of her gut was too small.

Are ill winds shaking
The fruit off your tree of faith?
Stay close to the trunk.

Bridget lifted her head, "Effey, why haven't we thought to pray?"

Aoife stretched out her mind hard and Lamentations 2:19 came to her, "*Rise during the night and cry out. Pour out your hearts like water to*

the Lord. Lift up your hands to him in prayer,
pleading for your children, for in every street they
are faint with hunger."

She began murmuring into Bridget's ear from deep inside. "Oh Biddy, our weakness must be God's weakness too. Lord, didn't you bleed and die in agony on the cross? Didn't you enter a darkness greater than ours without your father? Just like us, only more. Biddy, can you possibly imagine that?"

May your tears be mine.
As you die, watch me die too—
Your God be my God.

It must have been close to an hour—they prayed and suffered with Christ. "God was actually separated from himself, dead in darkness. My God! But Biddy, you know he arose from that death, right? Lord, you must have slain it like some fire-breathing dragon. I can just picture the battle. More like an execution. Oh praise you, our invincible God. And now your strength is our strength. So we lie limp in your hand, but strong forever and no one can snatch us away."

"Big big God," Bridget murmured. "You're holding me... my real daddy."

"And you're my loving and faithful bridegroom," Aoife purred. "More than enough. Overwhelming. Tender, more than mere manly care."

Eventually they were sleeping soundly, freed from all imaginary evils, with a host of angels standing guard against any real ones which might show up. It was well past first light when they awoke. Bridget, with a shaky hand, started to write a little story on a scrap of paper.

We were in a cave damp and dark. With one hope called a Bible. Hungy and pour. With a friend like a sister. Feeling sad and skard. Feeling Skard about Monsters called Pookus and black darkness. But before when I went in are storeye room I rememberd Monsters arn't reel there caricters in just made up Books. Jesus is stroyer than a Monster

The first item of business was to pour the contents of the bucket under the door. "Gardyloo," she muttered under her breath. As she was doing this, Aoife pictured part of herself draining away into some unseen gutter. Maybe next time it would be her blood.

**Functions of the flesh,
Fluids flowing everywhere—
Come soon King Jesus.**

"When will you be satisfied?" she cried out to God.

If you can believe it, a week went by like this. Lemon visited every evening with more food, water and reciting his poem.

3
For now, we'll call Him Poem Love,
His faith is ever true;
One graceful maestro majesty,
He's Word, and Song, and Hue.
"Forget me not," His name cries out,
Like family we will be;
He loves us, so He shows himself;
He speaks that we might see.
And with His breath He made Glowers,
Alive and crystal true,
They sing and dance and fly and prance,
And praise the Poem do.
And Poem loved them as they flew,
Throughout their wide expanse.

Lemon said the police were still searching for the girls and the fishermen were now carrying knives. It was far too dangerous to go out. A place to hide on a ship was hard to find, he reported, "Because the money wasn't right." Eventually,

Bridget was allowed to hold Scannalan, whom she found surprisingly soft. The animal seemed especially fond of climbing up her burlap smock to sniff through her hair. His long, scraggly whiskers tickled her ear. They became such good buddies that after a few days Lemon gave him to her. "I can get another one," he said. Aoife wasn't too sure about it, but the possum didn't eat much and was warm to cuddle at night. Also, it warded off any rats that might be about. And it ate big spiders they discovered.

By day, they napped and studied the Bible. By night, they meditated on it and prayed. It was all they had to do, but increasingly it was becoming enough. They were finding a mysterious joy and a strength outside themselves. After a while, the possum did indeed begin to smell, but the girls never noticed because they were in a similar state. No one cared. Not even their angels. In the darkness they not only stood guard but murmured reminders of things learned from the Bible.

Finally, the day came when Lemon forgot to lock the door behind him. The girls waited till dusk, then crept carefully out into the street. They carried only their blanket and their Bible. Scannalan rode nimbly on Bridget's shoulder. They didn't know they were leaping from the stewing pot onto the embers below.

Running and hiding;
The Lord is my hiding pace.
Ready or not, come.

The Seminary

In the far-off New World, within an old walled city, the ornate Cathedral-Basilica of Notre-Dame de Québec stood pompously and judgmentally over the diminutive Jean Marie Delacroix—just as it had over countless penitents since 1647. There was nowhere for him to hide. In the same city block, Le Petit Séminaire was less pretentiously ingesting young men for ordination as French-speaking priests. The thin man rose from his knees and walked through the garden to enrol. God could have his way. His graceful stride and flowery arm movements brandished an air of clerical robes. But his lapel flower was wilted. Nonetheless, he was an excellent student, religiously reciting his rosary and the Apostle's Creed:

> I believe in God, the Father Almighty,
> Creator of heaven and earth;
> and in Jesus Christ, His only Son, our Lord:
> Who was conceived by the Holy Ghost,
> born of the Virgin Mary;
> suffered under Pontius Pilate,
> was crucified, died and was buried.
> He descended into hell;
> the third day He rose again from the dead;
> He ascended into heaven,
> is seated at the right hand of God
> the Father Almighty;

from thence He shall come to judge
the living and the dead.
I believe in the Holy Ghost,
the Holy Catholic Church,
the communion of Saints,
the forgiveness of sins,
the resurrection of the body,
and life everlasting. Amen.

Occasionally, he stole out to visit his son at Saint Bridget's orphanage in nearby Sillery, as well as the boy's mother in Saint Patrick's cemetery not far down McMahon Street. The grave was common and unmarked. Piously, he would say an Act of Contrition over it.

O MY GOD,
I am heartily sorry for having offended Thee,
and I detest all my sins
because I dread the loss of Heaven
and the pains of Hell;
but most of all because they offend
Thee, my God, Who art all-good
and deserving of all my love.
I firmly resolve, with the help of Thy grace,
to confess my sins, to do penance,
and to amend my life. Amen.

He would chant this in three languages: French, English, and Latin—but wasn't really sorry at all.

Chapter 3

Rop tú mo chathscíath, rop tú mo chlaideb;
rop tussu m'ordan, rop tussu m'airer.
Rop tú mo dítiu, rop tú mo daingen;
rop tú nom-thocba i n-áentaid n-aingel.

Be thou my battle-shield, be thou my sword.
Be thou my dignity, be thou my delight.
Be thou my shelter, be thou my stronghold.
Mayst thou raise me up to the company of the angels.

The Inn

Free at last from the cellar, Aoife rushed
Bridget through the streets of Blarnybrae and along
the banks of Bungosteen Creek in a dimly lit
Muckanagheder Woods. Part of her didn't want to
return to the cottage at all, but to run away with the
sailor who had slipped fish under her smock. He
had kind eyes. But Bridget would be missing her
mother and needed to be home. Aoife had no home.
She thought about the three-masted sailing ships
that went to America. The sailor could take her
there and they could farm a small plot in gentle hills
by a trout stream. Their log cabin would have a
living room and a bedroom with a big brass bed.

And two goose down pillows with lace covers. Her dream became so real she stumbled over a root in the dim light. She reached out and almost pulled Scannalan off Bridget's shoulder.

"Are you all right?" her little sister asked.

"Very."

They continued on in a haze. It was quite dark when they reached the cottage—empty and chilling in the blue moonlight. The peat fire was out and cold. Aoife lit an oil lantern. She checked behind the loose brick and the money was gone. Perhaps the family had gone to visit relatives. Not likely. Bridget shuffled over and sat on her bed. Orange light danced on her ashen face.

"They have run away," she said.

"No, maybe they're in town; we'll check tomorrow. We should try to get some sleep now." Although there were plenty of empty beds, Aoife slept in her usual place on the straw in the corner by the fireplace. Bridget joined her there. They left the lamp on all night.

They must have been more tired than they'd thought because the sun was already high when they stirred. Bridget woke first with feelings of warmth and security in Aoife's arms. These lasted only seconds.

"Effey, wake up! We need to go find my family."

Aoife sat up groggily and straightened their hair with her comb-like fingers. They splashed water on their faces from a bucket. This was so refreshing they decided to take complete baths in the small pool of water behind the old rock wall. Scannalan got dunked in as well. Back at the cottage, they slipped into clean clothes but there was no food anywhere to be found.

"If we go to town now we'll be captured," Aoife said. "Best wait until evening." That gave them time to wash their clothes and hang them out to dry. Next, they did a complete search of the house and found a few coins, a tattered letter, a tin Claddagh ring, and a crumpled paper with the words "Notice to Quit" on it. By late afternoon, they had stuffed all these things along with some blankets into two burlap bags which could be carried over their shoulders. Before leaving, Aoife dusted and swept the floor.

Muckanagheder Woods seemed even more spooky than usual. There was a foul wind about and branches moved as if in pain, grabbing at hair and shoulders. The creek caught glimpses of moonlight and threw them back at the girls as if mud eels were spying from the depths. Scannalan hunkered down into Bridget's neck.

"Effey, the Pooka is nearby!"

"How do you know that?"

"My stomach is telling me."

"Oh that's just because you're hungry. We'll find something to eat in town."

Eventually they were out of the woods and hugging the walls of dark houses lining the alleys of Blarnybrae. They were attracted by some fiddles playing inside the back door of an unsavoury tavern dubbed Durty O'Musty's Inn. There were men laughing and cursing above the music but also the smell of fried food so they snuck right in.

"Sit right here in the corner," Aoife blew into Bridget's ear, "and get that animal into your bag."

The little girl pulled her blanket out and stuffed Scannalan in. The blanket she pulled over her head like a hood and hunched down at a small table in the shadows. Beautiful uilleann pipes (ILL-in) and a bodhrán drum (BOH-ron) were joining in. A crowd had gathered around them. There were no women to be seen. Everything in the bar was dark, glossy brown except the shiny brass fixtures and sparkly glasses. The wall behind the bar was lined with whiskey bottles and there was plenty of Guinness beer on tap. In front was a row of wide-rumped men teetering on high, rickety stools. Aoife left her bag with Bridget and squeezed her way in between two of them.

"Excuse me, sir," she addressed the barman, "but do you know anything about the whereabouts of my family, Paddy O'Day?"

"Hundreds go missing every day, Missy. You best be making your way outta here."

"Aw let her stay," piped up one of the drunks next to her. His elbow was in her ribs.

Aoife looked past his greasy neck and saw a brown-vested lounge boy approaching Bridget's table. Aoife scrambled over and sat down—leaving the man red-faced and shaking his fist.

"As I was telling sissy here," the boy said, "yous banshees not welcome here, but order your food and then get out. I amn't wantin' no trouble."

"Well, of course," said Aoife adjusting her cowl, "we'd like some nice bangers and mash. And tall glasses of milk." She jingled the coins in her pouch. When the boy looked doubtful she gave him her best smile. "And bring the milk right away."

The boy scurried off and in due course they were feasting off amazing plates of steaming sausages and potatoes. Many of the men in the

38

tavern were beginning to stare because ladies were not allowed in that part of the tavern and two skinny ghost-girls wearing blankets looked even more out of place. Also, one of the sacks beside them was beginning to move. Aoife removed everything suspicious and kicked the pile into the corner.

"Two shillings, six pence," the lounge boy reached out his hand to the older girl as they were finishing. She hesitated, then dumped her pouch onto the table. The small pile it made consisted mostly of farthings and a few hay-penny coins. She started counting it mournfully.

Just as the boy was turning away, a hand grabbed his shoulder and a rich baritone intoned, "It appears my daughters have brought the wrong purse again." The old man opened his gold velvet pouch, carefully selected one thin green wafer and presented it to the boy. He then tied it up with a drawstring braided from blond human hair. The boy looked up as if to question, but the man's gaze cut him off. "It will do," pronounced as if by some Druid priest.

Once they were safe outside the man threw back his cloak and began to whisper.

"Lemon!" exclaimed Bridget.

"Yes, it seems I'm here to rescue you again."

4
The best of these good Glowers strong,
Was flanking Poem Love,
When he did think himself quite cute,
For sure a cut above.
He spread his colours and his rays,
And fell in love with same.
They seemed to rival Poem's own;
It was a brand new game.

He sought to mock the Poem's Hue,
And sing a selfish tune.
But Love is just and called his dare,
So he'll be dead, and soon.
And with him went the third dragoon,
So now we call him Glare.

"Our parents have disappeared," Aoife said, "have you seen them?"

"Well, a three-master just left for Boston. I shouldn't wonder. Plenty of people can't pay rent and taxes. Landlords have to pay taxes themselves so it's cheaper to put the poor on ships just to get them off the land."

"Are the police still after us?" Bridget asked.

"No, sweet Alanna, I've taken care of all that. What's more I've a new home for yous."

"Where?" Aoife looked apprehensive.

"Number six, Dúghlas Road; you'll love it. Complete with real beds, meals and medical care. Come, I'll take you there. No obligation. You can leave anytime."

The Workhouse

It was a bit of a hike and the girls were tired when they finally stood at the big iron gate. Lemon gave the guard a green coin from his purse and they were admitted to the building itself. There Lemon gave two to the man in charge and the girls were told to sit on a bench out in the front hall. They held hands. "Hush," Aoife said:

1ˢᵗ Peter 4:19

Our pain—from his hand,
What our faithful Father planned.
So with him we stand.

Bridget added:

Only God's eternal outcome is known.

More than an hour later a matron emerged and led Bridget away down a dark hall. The little sister's eyes looked back pleadingly, but Aoife was too tired to protest or even react. It was cold. Her poor body was relieved just to flop down on a straw mattress in another part of the building. And faint away into blissful oblivion.

The stars shone as ice crystals that night and the wind whipped about like an assassin. Even night animals were content to be in their nests. Aoife awoke before dawn holding Bridget for warmth— but gradually realized it was not her little elf at all. It was someone larger and well, more developed. There was a lot more hair. The night was still dark, but Aoife stirred anyway and pushed the foreign body to arm's length.

"Sorry," it said.

"Who are you?" Aoife whimpered.

"Hush, you'll wake the others. Let me whisper in your ear."

Aoife stiffened but remained still.

"My name's Saoirse (SAIR-sha) and this is my bed. Almost all of us have to double up now. They say it's temporary."

"That's an unusual name," Aoife said. "What's it mean?"

"Freedom, haha. What's yours?"

"Aoife, means beauty, hahaha."

"I'm sure you're beautiful."

"Where are we?"

"Welcome to Saint Fubarr's Hospital and Workhouse. Stick close to me and I'll be your guide. They have lots of rules here. Don't break them."

"Do we have to work?"

"Some, and it's quite boring. Except when fights break out among the men."

"Are there any boys our age?"

Saoirse coughed quietly. "Just leave that alone. Now close your eyes and wait for the wake-up bell."

Breakfast was soda bread and water. They sat on benches at long plank tables, eight to a side. A sign over the doorway said, "GOD IS GOOD." Another read: "NOTICE—STRICT SILENCE and good order to be observed during MEAL TIME and NO FOOD TO BE REMOVED from the Dining Hall." Aoife noticed Saoirse was even skinnier than she, but her hair was longer—an impish, flaming carrot colour. In the wind, she would look like some great battle flag. Her eyes were a deep green flecked with gold. But most strikingly, her face was almost entirely freckles.

"They took my little sister away," Aoife said.

"They separate families; don't cha know. They're so cruel."

"Will I ever see her again?"

"There are ways. Just don't press it."

Come morning, Aoife found her bunkmate coughing over a toilet bowl. She helped her to a sink and cleaned up her face. The two were told to spend the day washing the sick and dying children in the hospital wing. Girls were used because they could be of special comfort. They found one small boy already dead in diarrhoea and vomit. Aoife stared blankly into Saoirse's eyes. What if this had been Biddy lying there?

"You'll get used to things here. Come on, let's get 'im cleaned up and dressed for burial. The boys dig new holes every day." When they had finished with everyone they mopped the floor and took the dirty sheets to the laundry room. Other girls were there to boil them clean. Then they washed themselves in the big open shower room. Saoirse just stood there shivering under a dribble of cold water from her pipe. Aoife looked down at the dirty water trickling between the older girl's toes and through the slats of the wooden floor. Saoirse shook her hair like a dog and giggled. "Oh for a warm towel," she said. After that they went outside under a tree for some idle time before dinner.

"Wait, let me go get my Bible," Aoife said. They sat on a bench and opened it together. "Don't you hate this place?" she asked her new friend.

"It's a place to survive. The boys tell me life is better as a prisoner in county gaol. The food is better there and there's fewer rules."

Aoife grimaced and began to read in Job 6:4-11.

> "*For the Almighty has struck me down with his*
>   *arrows.*
> *Their poison infects my spirit.*
> *God's terrors are lined up against me.*

Don't I have a right to complain?
Don't wild donkeys bray when they find no
grass,
and oxen bellow when they have no food?
Don't people complain about unsalted food?
Does anyone want the tasteless white of an
egg?
My appetite disappears when I look at it;
I gag at the thought of eating it!
"Oh, that I might have my request,
that God would grant my desire.
I wish he would crush me.
I wish he would reach out his hand and kill
me.
At least I can take comfort in this:
Despite the pain,
I have not denied the words of the Holy One.
But I don't have the strength to endure.
I have nothing to live for.

"Sometimes I feel that way," Saoirse said.

"Me too. How do you cope?"

"I have an inner path and a guide who helps keep me on it; do you want to know more?"

Aoife blinked at her. "I have this book that's a lamp unto my feet."

Saoirse smiled. "Like me. We'll have to talk more tomorrow. Now's time for supper."

The meal, as always, was called "stirabout." Typically it was a porridge of oat or cornmeal and a meagre portion of whatever else might be available: fish, pork, rabbit, or leftover breakfast. Aoife wondered if possum would do. After this, they washed dishes and cleaned the dining room until it was time to fall into bed. There were about twenty-five cots lined up in the room, each with two chamber pots neatly placed underneath. Sure enough, Aoife observed two slim girls slipping into each bed.

The evening routine never changed much. Aoife did find time to inspect the tattered letter from the cottage. It was just an old envelope soiled with soot. She could barely make out the return address: 138 St. Ja--s Av---e, Bos--n, Ma------setts, Uni-----------f Amer--a.

The Mill

Next day all the girls took the first shift at the Capstan Mill which produced whole-meal flour from wheat, and Indian meal from corn. This was for the workhouse bread. Aoife and Saoirse walked side-by-side in a great circle, pushing one of twenty-four iron poles sticking out from a central capstan, which by a series of shafts and gears turned a set of millstones. They worked for an hour till their calves ached. Then forty-eight women took over for two hours, then the boys for three, and the men for five. Thus the mill was operated about 11 hours per day. After their stint, the girls were returned to other duties. Aoife and Saoirse again bathed the sick and buried the dead. There was no formal education, but Saoirse said she had learned to weave and spin in years past.

That afternoon during free time, the two girls found their bench under the tree and opened the Bible.

"How do you handle the stress here?" Aoife asked.

"I just empty my mind and peace comes."

"Well look at this," Aoife said turning to Romans 5:3-5.

"We can rejoice, too, when we run into problems and trials, for we know that they help us develop endurance. And endurance develops strength of character, and character strengthens our confident hope of salvation. And this hope will not lead to disappointment. For we know how dearly God loves us, because he has given us the Holy Spirit to fill our hearts with his love.

"Is this Holy Spirit your Spirit Guide?" Saoirse asked.

"No, he's more than a guide, he's my whole life," Aoife said. "I live for him. He lives in me."

"Creepy. Well it doesn't seem like he's treating you very well—doesn't appear you're very free."

"I know," said Aoife bowing her head a little. At times, she wondered why she couldn't fully believe what she knew to be true. Saoirse took her hand and they walked over to dinner.

"I'll be your Spirit Guide and show you true freedom," she said.

Aoife replied, "And I'll lead you to Christ who is the way, the truth and the life."

That night Saoirse left the bed and was gone for hours. "Where were you?" Aoife asked.

"Just leave that alone. Now close your eyes and wait for the wake-up bell."

This happened two or three times a week, so one night Aoife asked if they could visit Bridget. At first Saoirse frowned but then took her arm and led past the bathroom, up to the third floor where the small girls slept. They tiptoed past bunk after bunk until Aoife recognized her sister. She was sleeping with Scannalan.

"Creepy," said Saoirse.

Bridget stirred and Aoife put a finger on her small lips. "How are you, Biddy? Are you doing okay?"

Bridget sat up and hugged her. "Oh Effey, I hate it here. There're so many rules and I miss Mamaí (MAH-mee)."

"Is the work too hard for you?"

"Oh no, I'm even learning to sew. But some of the girls are mean."

"How come you get to keep that weasel?" Saoirse asked.

"I don't," said Bridget. "He disappears into the attic by day. He knows just where to find food by night and then comes to cuddle me for a while. And he's not a weasel."

"Well, be careful," Aoife said, "or he'll end up in the supper stirabout. Lucky you don't have a bed mate like me." She glanced at Saoirse who wrinkled her nose.

"Effey, I want to go home and live with you again."

"I know. Me too. Maybe someday soon. Can we be praying for that?"

"I can trust God," Bridget said.

They left her wiping away tears, but visited whenever they could. Saoirse was often tired from her other night excursions but never disclosed details. Aoife suspected she was seeing a boy but had no idea how that could happen. The boys and men were downstairs on the ground floor and crammed in even tighter than girls. Besides none of them seemed even remotely attractive.

48

The Oakum Girl

The great sailing ships of the day were made of wood planks caulked watertight with a mixture of tar and loose fibre, obtained by untwisting old rope. This fibre was called oakum and the next morning the girls were set to the laborious task of oakum picking—unravelling the stiff cords into loose piles. They sat in neat rows, all in their drab grey dresses tied at the waist, and nearly identical, dirty white bonnets. There was no talking or gaiety of any kind; they were supposed to keep their eyes down at their work. Even so, Saoirse poked Aoife with her elbow occasionally to cheer her up. But when their eyes met they found only stagnant pools. They toiled like this with bare hands until fingers became numb, scratched and cramping. Each girl was expected to produce one pound. Aoife was a bit short the first day but the girl seated behind her kicked some extra under her chair and that made up the difference. All that girl received in return was a sweet smile but it seemed enough somehow. Later she would receive more.

Yes, that afternoon this oakum girl followed Aoife and Saoirse out to the bench under the tree.

"My name's Einin (EH-neen)," she said shyly, "may I sit with you?"

"Yes, of course," said Saoirse, "I'm showing Aoife here the path to freedom, and she's showing me what's in her little black book."

Aoife opened it to 2nd Timothy 3:16 and passed it to Einin. "Oakum picking unravels, but the Bible weaves everything together."

*All Scripture is inspired by God and is useful to
teach us what is true and to make us realize what is
wrong in our lives. It corrects us when we are
wrong and teaches us to do what is right.*

Saoirse seemed uncomfortable with this. "My
path tells me the free choices I love are always
right." Einin's eyes, however, remained riveted to
Aoife's Bible. They turned the pages back to
Matthew 4:1-4.

Aoife spoke again, "We grind flour but man
does not live by bread alone."

*Then Jesus was led by the Spirit into the
wilderness to be tempted there by the devil. For
forty days and forty nights he fasted and became
very hungry.
During that time the devil came and said to
him, "If you are the Son of God, tell these stones to
become loaves of bread."
But Jesus told him, "No! The Scriptures say,
'People do not live by bread alone,
but by every word that comes from the mouth of
God.'"*

"My spirit guide would never lead me into
temptation," Saoirse said. "All things are
permitted."
Aoife glanced at her, "If your god lets you do
anything you want, then your god must be you."
She read 1st John 4:1.

*Dear friends, do not believe everyone who
claims to speak by the Spirit. You must test them to*

see if the spirit they have comes from God. For there are many false prophets in the world.

Saoirse and Aoife stared at each other. The former had great passion and sincerity, but the latter had a stronger power standing behind her. Aoife loved her friend. "Here we bury the dead but the Bible shows us how to get new life. 2nd Corinthians 5:17 says:"

This means that anyone who belongs to Christ has become a new person. The old life is gone; a new life has begun!

"The Bible does not free us from workhouse bondage," she continued, "but from slavery to sin and Satan. Romans 6:18."

Now you are free from your slavery to sin, and you have become slaves to righteous living.

She looked over into Saoirse's puppy-like face. "Could it be your god is lying to you, promising a freedom that doesn't satisfy in the end? Galatians 3:22."

But the Scriptures declare that we are all prisoners of sin, so we receive God's promise of freedom only by believing in Jesus Christ.

Saoirse stiffened and crossed her arms in challenge. But Aoife rested her hand on them, "You will surely die on this path. Galatians 5:13." Her eyes moistened and she held her gaze.

For you have been called to live in freedom, my brothers and sisters. But don't use your freedom to satisfy your sinful nature. Instead, use your freedom to serve one another in love.

Saoirse said, "It seems like you're asking me to exchange one form of slavery for another."

"Only Jesus can be the holy salt in your life," Aoife said. "He doesn't enslave but brings out and preserves your true flavour and frees you from your bondage to conformity in sin. Who but he can restore you to everything you were meant to be? And preserve you, my unique and beautiful Saoirse."

After that day Einin brought several other girls to the little afternoon Bible study but in a few weeks the workhouse authorities shut it down because it wasn't following the proper Catholic catechism. Still, it made lasting impressions on many and new excitement about Jesus spread. Colossians 4:6.

Let your speech always be with grace, as though seasoned with salt, so that you will know how you should respond to each person. (NASB)

Einin was especially affected. Her happy smile could be seen everywhere. It was as if she were drifting through life on some fluffy, pink cloud— even on the hardest workdays. She kept kicking oakum under Aoife's chair, even when she herself was short for that day. Not that trials had suddenly ended for Einin. If anything they increased. She was small and her ears pointed out like an elf. Some of the bigger girls started picking on her. Her inner peace only incensed them more. They were jealous of her apparent power over more and more young people. She was shoved in the halls and pinched when they sat together in their neat rows. They began stealing most of her food. She refused to fight back, however, yet was often punished as an instigator.

One night when Saoirse was away, she hobbled over and slipped into bed with Aoife. "Oh, the most amazing thing has happened to me," she whispered. "I got so sad about my—sin—my heart wept and cried out to Jesus. Before, I wasn't turning to him. I was too proud." Here her voice broke and she just sobbed into Aoife's shoulder. "Oh Effey, I was mean to him but he changed me anyway. His Spirit came inside me. He loves me so much it's scary. Now I know I'm really free, and free forever. I know it. I believe it. I love him."

Aoife's lips touched her hair.

"*Bígí láidir*," said the small one in her arms, "be strong." There was a pause as her breath quickened and they breathed in unison. Einin's last words before falling asleep were: "*Mar is é Críost is beatha domsa agus ba shochar dom an bás.*" "To live is Christ, to die is gain," from Philippians 1:21. Then she became peaceful.

A tear appeared in Aoife's eye. God was truly mighty and merciful. What new and wonderful things would he be doing with his new child? When Saoirse returned they found sweet Einin, the one who clung to every page of Aoife's Bible, had passed on from Aoife's arms into those of her Jesus. Einin, whose name means "little bird," had flown from a cruel earth up into the only true and eternal freedom.

But this did not make Aoife very happy at all. Their Einin was gone and that hurt. God was not being nice or fair. Saoirse tried to comfort her, "She's not dead so long as she lives in our hearts."

Yet Aoife didn't fully understand until their next visit to Bridget when the young sister asked, "But don't you think it makes Jesus happy to bring her to heaven to be with himself?"

Death, just the door to eternity.

The next afternoon who should appear under the tree but Lenna Ó Leannáin himself. "Colleen girl, how have you been? I fret about you every day. But our salvation is at hand."

"How is that?" Aoife asked. Saoirse was staring wide-eyed at what she perceived must be a wizard or a Druid priest ranting.

5
Yes Poem Love did speak a world,
A time to pace it in.
And with it came a light and night,
And days and skies begin.
So next He split the land from sea,
To make the green Feed grow.
Then in the sky cast lights and stars,
And all was good, you know.
So after that came Pets for us,
To tend and care for well.
All kinds that run and fly and swim,
Some beautiful, some smell.
And with them on the world we dwell,
All glory be to Him.

Aoife added this:

God spoke creation;
He made everything but light—
Because God IS light.

"I've procured passage to the promised land for you and your sister," Lemon hesitated, "and your pretty friend here too, of course. Only just now has the price become acceptable. At last, there is new life for yous. Freedom."

Aoife felt her heart thumping at her ribs and her stomach leaped. Her mouth became dry. "Passage" could only mean a tall ship.

"Truly?" she asked with puppy eyes. "Can you really get us out of here?"

"I got you in, didn't I?" said Lemon. "So where is my dear child Alanna and her wee Scannalan?"

"They won't be available until late tonight."

"I can wait right here; we'll depart at first light."

Aoife replied:

Others chase the sun,
Escape on colour arcs—
I await the dawn.

"We'll meet you then. Saoirse can you be ready?"

Saoirse's face fell and she bowed her head. "Oh Aoife, I'm not free to go. Not free at all. You may have the Holy Spirit inside you, but my heart binds me here." She put Aoife's hand on her belly. Her eyes glistened in the afternoon sunshine and a tear trickled through the maze of freckles on her cheek. "I don't know my path, loving sister, but I'm not alone to choose. Yet I know one thing is true: your god IS God. But I just can't."

The Ordination

Jean Marie Delacroix had decided he could. He could go through his approaching ordination ceremony with purely humanitarian motives. God to him, was an empty cathedral—Notre-barren-Dame de Québec—a shell, all plaster and mortar—filled only with tombs and dead words. Dead like the bones of Saint François de Laval, first bishop of New France, namesake of the Université Laval nearby. Jean wondered if it would have a medical school to heal the body as well as the soul. Actually, he doubted if God could do either.

So he would lie about his faith in order to serve mankind. At the ceremony, the bishop asked, "Do you resolve to be united more closely every day to Christ the High Priest, who offered himself for you to the Father as a pure Sacrifice, and with him to consecrate yourself to God for the salvation of all?"

"I do, with the help of God," Jean lied. He then knelt before the great gold-threaded robe and placed his joined hands between its outstretched ones.

"Do you promise to respect and obey me and my successors?" continued the stiff vestment.

"I do," Jean lied again, anxious to be about the business of helping people—at least the French-speaking ones. And most particularly not the Irish immigrants who were crawling all over the land like snakes. A most ironic notion.

Then the bishop pronounced, "This man who now, through this Sacrament of Holy Orders, has become a priest, participates in Christ's priesthood; he acts *in persona Christi Capitis*, in the person of Christ, the Head of His Body, the Church. May God, who has begun this good work in him bring it to fulfilment."

"Amen," said Jean, lying the third time as he thought he perceived a cock crowing faintly in the distance.

As fortune would have it, this was an Extraordinary Jubilee Year called by the church to receive special blessing and pardon for sins from God. This particular cathedral had a *Porta Sancta*, or Holy Door, normally bricked up from the inside but now open for pilgrims to enter and piously gain plenary indulgences. In Luke 11:9 Jesus said, "*Keep on asking, and you will receive what you ask for. Keep on seeking, and you will find. Keep on knocking, and the door will be opened to you.*" The Holy Door is the passageway from sin to holiness, a visual symbol of internal renewal, beginning with the willing desire to reconcile with God, make peace with neighbours, and heal the wounded heart through conversion. At least that was Jean Marie Delacroix's understanding of what he had been taught at Le Petit Séminaire.

Indulgences, he learned, take away all or part of the temporal punishment still due to sin. "Temporal punishment" means that even though all sins are forgiven in Confession and eternal punishment in hell is taken away, God still demands punishment for a time, either in this life or in Purgatory. The Church has authority from Jesus Christ to discipline and draw on the spiritual bank of his merits, along with his Mother's and the Saints'. *"And I will give you the keys of the Kingdom of Heaven. Whatever you forbid on earth will be forbidden in heaven, and whatever you permit on earth will be permitted in heaven."* Matthew 16:19.

Jean Marie Delacroix rose and genuflected on his way out the holy door—the wrong way, from the side with Mary on it, forgetting to make the sign of the cross, but enjoying his new flowing robe, flowery hat, and fresh title. Father. The rarefied air was heady in his nostrils.

He headed down the street to find a carriage to visit his son before enrolling in Université Laval Faculté de Médecine. Buzzing in his head was Martin Luther's 32nd Thesis, *"Those who suppose that on account of their letters of indulgence they are sure of salvation will be eternally damned along with their teachers."* And his 36th, *"Every Christian who truly repents has plenary, full forgiveness both of punishment and guilt bestowed on him, even without letters of indulgence."* And finally his 95th, *"Let Christians experience problems if they must—and overcome them—rather than live a false life based on present Catholic teaching."*

Jean thought he knew all about problems but he'd find there were others far more entangled in them than he.

Chapter 4

Rop tú cech maithius dom churp, dom anmain;
rop tú mo flaithius i n-nim 's i talmain.
Rop tussu t' áenur sainserc mo chride;
ní rop nech aile acht Airdrí nime.

Be thou every good to my body and soul.
Be thou my kingdom in heaven and on earth.
Be thou solely chief love of my heart.
Let there be none other, O high King of Heaven.

The Cave

So by her own choices Saoirse, whose name means freedom, left herself behind in bondage. As Matthew 7:13 says, *"You can enter God's Kingdom only through the narrow gate. The highway to hell is broad, and its gate is wide for the many who choose that way."*

Also Hebrews 6:4-6.

For it is impossible to bring back to repentance those who were once enlightened—those who have experienced the good things of heaven and shared in the Holy Spirit, who have tasted the goodness of the word of God and the power of the age to come— and who then turn away from God. It is impossible to bring such people back to repentance; by rejecting the Son of God, they themselves are nailing him to the cross once again and holding him up to public shame.

To be completely free, we must want happiness, be able to achieve it, and in the end be satisfied forever, never abandoned. Saoirse was unable. Only Jesus can make this happen. Remember what Einin was able to quote, *"To live is Christ; to die is gain."*

So if the Son sets you free, you are truly free. John 8:36.

Lenna Ó Leannáin headed toward the docks with Aoife and Bridget in tow. He said it was too dangerous to go through town so they made directly for the ocean and followed the coastline.

Hermit crabs were everywhere. They saw a fairly large empty snail shell and twenty crabs lined up next to it, in order from largest to smallest. Soon a big crab happened by and decided to move into the large roomier shell—leaving its old shell vacant. Immediately all the crabs switched shells in turn, each one moving up to the next size, leaving only the smallest shell on the sand. Bridget picked it up.

"Don't build your house on the sand," Lemon said. "Don't sleep there either with hermit crabs around; they'll back into your ears, latch on to your eardrums, and control your hearing." He scattered them with his foot.

At the base of the cliffs, Lemon ducked into an all but invisible cleft in the rock and squeezed through an impossibly small opening into a hidden cave. The others, being thinner and smaller had little trouble following.

"We must wait here until evening to board the ship," he said. They were in a small, semi-dark chamber with moisture dripping down rough walls and the rhythmic sound of surf muffled in the background. The air was heavy. "I'm ancient, you know. Older than you think. But I'm not suffered to die until I recite my entire poem to a maiden red rosebud:

6
All glory to Him in endless rhyme,
Not bound by space or time;
Beyond the alpha omega,
(The original paradigm.)
Love not bound by understanding,
A presence everywhere,
A knowledge complete and profound,
With wisdom just and fair.
His creation pictures perfection,
But not as great as He;
With vast and cosmic shape imbued,
But not as big as He.
We're given eyes to dimly see,
Love's great infinitude.

"Is that about God?" the girls wondered. Aoife said:

Wind blows over ground—
Till Christ's great name be renowned,
There's no grave for us.

Bridget:

Finding God in our darkest caves

She dug out a candle from her sack and asked Lemon for a light.

"You little candle-flies," he said, "be careful not to inspect your God beyond what is revealed, lest pride overcome you and he singe your pretty powdery wings and dash you to earth.

O bright round faun eyes,
Avoiding my fading ones—
Mine, you soon will have.

"Lemon, you're a buzzing dumbledore," said Bridget, "we're not dumb moths." But Aoife looked away.

"So what do we do now?" she asked.

"We dig." He indicated a small depression in the cave floor. "We can start here."

All they could find outside were big, flat clam shells, so while they scraped sand, the old man told them a story. "Once many years ago there was an Irish pirate queen named Gráinne O'Malley. Let's just call her Grace. She was very wealthy and controlled many ships. One day she was running from several English men-of-war and ducked in here under cover of a fog bank. Legend has it she left a chest of gold, intending to pick it up later, but never did."

"How do you know all this?" Aoife asked.

Lemon produced a small piece of rumpled parchment.

"A treasure map!" exclaimed Bridget.

"Actually it's a bookmark. My grandfather, Athair Mór gave it to me just before he died. The book itself was burned in a fire and discarded decades ago. But the heat transferred some ink to this strip and it survived over these many years. Indeed, see this faint outline. It was barely sufficient to locate this place."

Sure enough, Aoife could make something out, even in the subdued light. In due course they began scraping wood instead of sand and it wasn't long before they had unearthed an ornately carved, but battered and rotting box. It was small, about the size of a dead man's chest. Inside they found not gold but dirt. "Looks like it was dug up before," Lemon said, "more's the pity."

As they were putting it back, Bridget noticed a brief glint of green light blinking out of the hole. Aoife dropped the box on it and kicked sand on top.

"No wait!" said Bridget and her little arms hauled it out again. "I saw something."

"It must have fallen out and been overlooked when the chest was first opened," Lemon said, retrieving a dainty necklace with his skeleton-like fingers. Excitedly they blew sand off to reveal a fine gold chain with a green pendant the size of a bean. A large bean—but teardrop shaped and very sparkly. It actually glowed in the dim light. They rushed outside. There it caught the sun's fire—in deep emerald green but brilliantly radiating all

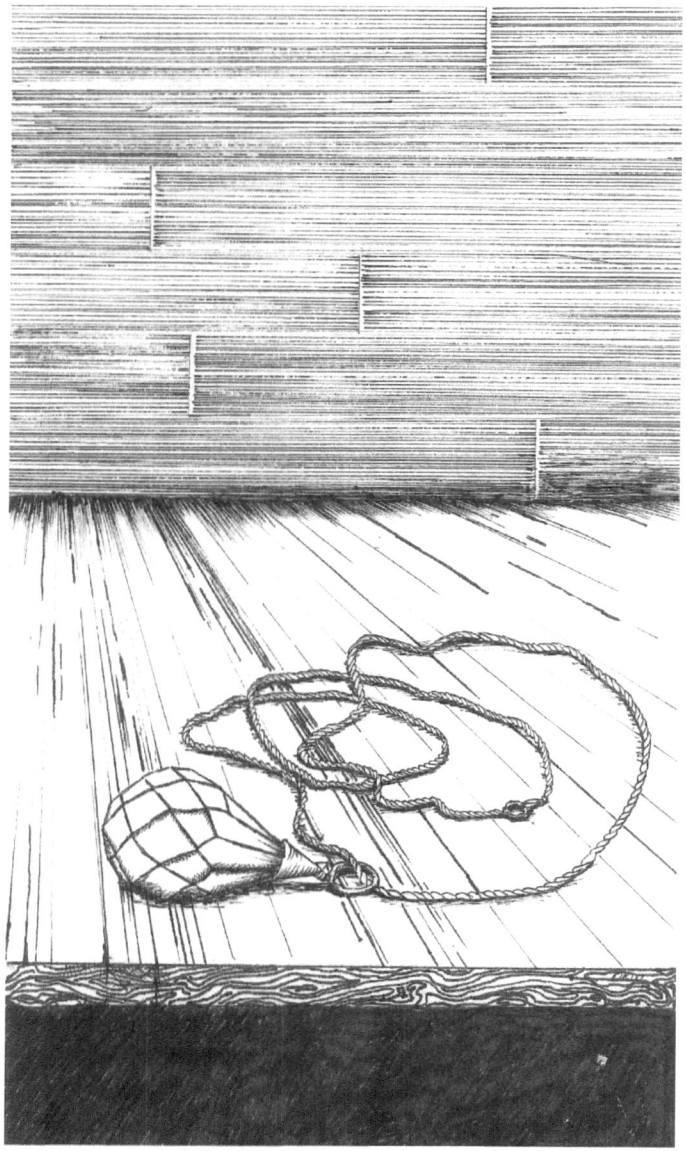

colours of the rainbow from its facets. "This could be something of very great value," Lemon said. "I've never seen anything like it. Where can we keep it best hidden?" He thought of his lucky charm purse but then gently clasped the jewel around Aoife's neck. "Nobody will molest it here," he said. Resting on her smock, it set off her red hair impressively. She had never possessed such a thing of beauty. "Now tuck it safely inside." She was surprised how well it could hide, nicely nestled down her tiny front.

"I'll keep it safe and warm," she thought to herself. As a girl, she felt precious for the first time in her life. When they were leaving the cave Bridget glanced about one last time but clearly there were to be no jewels for her.

The Ship

Walking along just before sunset the first thing they glimpsed was a long colourful pennant flowing from the main royal of the tall ship *Agnes*. Its three great masts grew impressively on the ground as the trio approached the stern like bugs across tree shadows. The lower main and foremast yardarms had been angled down by the cock-up crew so as not to interfere with other ships' rigging or dock equipment.

There was a lot of activity on the wharf with people wrestling trunks and satchels. Old folks were sitting on wooden boxes, snapping at kids racing about on the hot gravel. A guardsman stood on the docks, blocking the gangplank and checking papers.

Of course, Lemon had none. "Don't worry," he told the man, "I have a special agreement with Captain McCrawly." But not with the guard apparently. It took them three lucky charms to board the vessel.

"What were those?" Bridget asked.

"Connemara marble," he said, "and a wee bit of charm." He grinned and put a finger to his lips.

They made their way aft and down to the captain's quarters. No one stopped them because they seemed to know where they were going. The captain was out so they sat down at his little table and waited. The ship's logbook was on the table, along with a dip pen and inkwell. *The Ship Agnes* was inscribed at the top of every page.

"Look girls," Lemon said, "the logbook says *Agnes* but I must change its name to *Agnes Dei*.

"Why in heaven's name?" Aoife asked.

"Because red-headed women bring very bad luck to a ship unless the name is immediately changed," Lemon replied.

"Biddy," Aoife said, "hide that animal in your bag before it spills ink on that book. That's what would bring the bad luck, not our hair."

Lemon continued, "Do you know it's called a 'logbook,' because records were originally inscribed on shingles cut from logs, then bound so they opened like books. The girls looked disinterested and tired; he was relieved when the grey-haired officer entered a few moments later.

"Is this the young lady?" the captain asked in a gravelly voice.

"Yes," said Lemon, "as agreed." They all stood up.

"Pretty, but skinnier than most," the captain said.

"But gaining," Lemon replied. Aoife had in fact filled out a bit. Even workhouse stirabout was better than the potato water of the cottage. Also she was becoming more shapely. The captain's eyes made her self-conscious and she reached to finger the necklace, but remembered to keep it secret. Keep it safe. It made her feel precious.

"A deal," the captain said, handing Lemon a packet of paper money. "And you'll take care of the little one?"

"As agreed," said Lemon.

"Go find a bunk for them, well forward by the fo'c'sle, and only one. We've all the souls we can carry this trip. You sleep aft." Every ship was limited by U.S. law as to number of passengers based on its size. Britain allowed fifty percent more so the *Agnes Dei* was headed to British North America. Even so, it was quite adept at accommodating additional stowaways. Below decks were rows and rows of wooden platforms which served as bunks, living quarters and hiding places. Crude benches and tables were fashioned amidships. The cookhouse was above decks and in case of fire the whole thing could be tossed overboard, cast-iron stove and all. Fire was such a hazard on wooden ships that any flames were carefully controlled. A "smoking lamp" was lit from time to time in the forecastle (FOKE-sul) forward part of the ship below deck, just outside the crew's living quarters. It was the only way to light cigarettes. None of the newly invented matches were permitted and smoking was banned in all sleeping areas.

The companionway, or stairs down was impossibly steep, almost a ladder with rungs slick and worn by countless oily feet. The girls eased their way below and dragged themselves to a narrow bunk. Lemon sat on the lower, leaving the girls to hoist themselves into the upper. There was no ladder. Scannalan, they tucked in a nook near the ceiling. Lemon stared at Aoife and began to recite:

7
Then We shall make a Race He said,
To shine and image Us.
So from the dust He formed him well—
Results were fabulous.
Of Sōma, Psychē and Pneuma made,
He breathed in facets three.
The Feed had one, the Pets but two,
Now Race too spirit be.
To talk with Poem and love him well,
And tend his Feed and Pets.
The Feed were food for them to eat,
The Pets emotive outlets.
Race did ask, "Is this as good as loving gets?
I still feel incomplete."

It was dark but not late. Nevertheless, the girls were asleep shortly after Lenna Ó Leannáin ambled aft.

Early next morning Aoife woke first, disturbed that the workhouse was rocking. But they were at sea! Bridget stirred in her arms and they peered from beneath their blanket.

"Son of a gun, we're at sea," Aoife said.

70

Lemon was sitting at a table nailed to the centre of their deck. "Curious, you know that's an expression for children born of girls brought on board by sailors in port. The men had no private quarters so they slung hammocks between the cannons to sleep in." The girls paid no attention to him. "Come on, I'm just having coffee and a biscuit. I'm bunking at the rear of the ship. It's all girls up here, I'm afraid."

There were lumps in all the other beds, but no one else was moving. The two girls slipped down and helped themselves to some soda bread, and water from the scuttlebutt, a wooden cask containing the ship's daily ration. A ladle with small holes in it hung alongside. That was to discourage lingering over one's water allotment.

"In the old days and even now," Lemmon said, "if you steal water you'll be keelhauled. They tie a rope to each of your arms and shove you off the bow of the ship under sail. Then you're dragged under the ship along its barnacle encrusted keel—to be pulled aboard at the stern, half alive."

There was no coffee. Later they found they were permitted only one pound of food per day, almost starvation rations.

Aoife rubbed her eyes and stared at Lemon. "Am I missing something or did you sell me to the captain last night?" She cocked her head and fingered the neckline of her chemise.

Why do I fear men,
And trust my earthly trinkets?
Who's my Lord, O heart?

"Oh that, no worries. There's no funny business. You have workhouse nursing experience.

71

In exchange for our passage, you take care of the sick on the voyage. There's no ship's doctor. But no one will get sick. Maybe a few cuts and scratches. Now I better move aft before any of these lassies begin rousing." He took an extra biscuit with him.

Bridget rolled over and poked Aoife.

Wise girls don't trust Pooka shenanigans

Scannalan crept down from the rafters, across the girls' bunk, and then over the sleeping body below. Bridget grabbed him immediately but not before the girl opened her eyes and whimpered, "Is that a rat?"

"Oh no, it's Mister O'possom, and he's my pet."

"It doesn't bite," Aoife added.

"Well, it sure is ugly," the girl said, crossing herself.

"With that I must agree. My name's Aoife, and this here's Bridget."

"And Scannalan," said Bridget.

"Well, I'm Caitlín (KAHT-leen)," the girl said, swinging her bare feet to the floor. She was wearing an embroidered silk nightgown which had been white in better times. She cinched it loosely at the waist. A small crucifix on a fine gold chain graced her neck. Her face was not gaunt like the others and her eyes were star sapphires.

"He eats rats," Bridget said, "and anything else you can think of, even spiders and rotting things. See how he climbs? It's like he has thumbs on his hind legs. He'll hide during the day."

"I'd like to see it hang from its tail," Caitlín said. Her princess nose was slightly turned up at the creature. Or maybe it was always turned up.

"Oh he doesn't do that, but he can hang on to branches with it."

"Well, it does look cute with those black elvish ears," Caitlín said. "You should inform the crew so they don't kill it. Tell them it brings good luck." When Aoife looked puzzled she added, "They live right behind that door over there. Go right in. They're friendly."

Aoife hesitated, then went over and knocked timidly.

"Just peek in," Caitlín said, peering impishly at Bridget. "They get up early." Bridget covered her eyes.

The door opened just a crack, but that was enough to behold the figure of hairy, muscular legs stepping into trousers. Aoife gasped and pulled back from the door, unintentionally slamming it. She turned wildly, only to see Caitlin and Bridget stifling giggles.

"Biddy, I'll wring your neck."

"She did it!" her sister sniggered.

Aoife stared at Caitlín with a saccharin smile. She'd have fun paying her back for this. All three girls were sitting on her bunk when the man emerged, all clean and cute and covered. He wore white bell-bottom trousers which could be rolled up easily when swabbing the deck. And a billowy white shirt with a black neckerchief tied neatly in front with a square knot. Despite a full beard and moustache, he had a boyish look. All his hair was swept up to one side like short grass blown by some great sea gale. It was a dreamy chocolate brown. His nose was long, thin as a ship's rudder and slightly red at the tip. His eyes were gunmetal blue and his hands resembled old gloves. He was, in fact, the perfect picture of a craggy old sea dog, yet as a puppy.

All the girls seemed impressed but only Aoife knew of the many muscles under his sailor suit. She recognized something else as well but kept shyly silent though her insides were about to burst. He looked straight ahead and bounded directly and deftly up the stairs, two at a time.

"Biddy," Aoife said, "that's the fisherman on the dock that I—I mean that we…" her voice trailed off. She brushed hair out of her face.

"Really? He must have got a new job," Bridget said. "By the way, where's the toilet?"

"It's called 'the head,'" Caitlín interjected, "because it's located forward, below our deck, close to the figurehead, even though we don't have one of those. It drains just above the water line so waves can wash it clean."

"In the bow?" Bridget asked. "Wouldn't that stink up the whole ship?"

"A sailor told me it's actually downwind of everything because the winds push the ship from behind."

"Well however it works, can we get there soon, Effey?"

They spent the rest of the day exploring the hold of the ship and meeting people. There were families, some complete with babies and grandparents. Sisters, cousins, and aunts. There were quite a few single girls: Aileen, Brianna, Claire, Daireann, Enda, Fiona, Gael, and so on, to put them in order. Aoife meant to know them all by next morning. Scuttlebutt had it there were 490 souls on board. That was the official tally anyway, including the assorted sailors who paraded through the girls into crew quarters before the mast. Ordinary seamen lived in the bow of the ship, in front of the foremast. They came and went all day but Aoife noticed hers was not among them. Was he avoiding her?

There was no place to undress. The first thing she learned was to change behind a blanket which they strung between two bunks. She thought she had better put on her best frock, she only had two, before venturing on deck. As she was undressing Caitlín noticed her pendant.

"Oh, that's a pretty green stone you're wearing, where'd you get it?"

"It's been in the family. It's nothing, just green amber."

"You know, diamonds and sapphires can be green. It might be valuable." Caitlín could see even from a distance it wasn't just amber. "That's an old briolette cut," she said, and the gold chain looks Elizabethan. Let me show you something. She reached into her sack and pulled out a ring, heavy with diamonds. "See these hidden spaces under the bezel," she said, "back then the ladies hid scented wax to mask bad body odour. Even the finest of ladies hated the bath. They were deemed unsanitary. A ring could be brought up to the nose whenever a smell became too much to endure."

"Where do we bathe here?" Bibby asked.

The three just grinned at each other.

The Sailor

Only twenty people were allowed on deck at a time—to breathe fresh air, rinse out their clothing in saltwater, and clean themselves as best they could. On one such occasion, the elusive fisherman happened to catch Aoife alone on a starboard gangway. She had rested her Bible, Psalm 8 open on the railing and was enjoying the last colour of sunset.

³ When I look at the night sky and see the work of your fingers—
>*the moon and the stars you set in place—*
⁴ what are mere mortals that you should think about them,
>*human beings that you should care for them?*

She got a splinter in her thumb while stroking the rail but quickly pulled it out. She was sucking on it when he spoke over her shoulder.

"I'm sorry," he said. "A splinter's called a 'shiver.' That's where 'shiver me timbers' comes from."

She spat out her thumb. "Don't be sorry." Her cheeks were flushed as the sunset.

"I'm Faolan (FWAIL-awn) Rogan. Do I know you from somewhere?"

"You once gave me a fish."

"Oh you. You and your little daughter." He smiled.

"My sister."

"Uh. And you—are?"

"I'm Aoife O'Day."

"Pleased to make your acquaintance, Miss Day. I'm sorry about my boss. He sacked me because of you."

"I'm sorry."

"I hated sorting fish anyway."

"Nice evening," Aoife said, "do you see the stars coming out? Such nice weather."

"It's going to storm," Faolan said, "Yesterday I saw seagulls flying inland."

"Maybe they were just hungry. What are all these ropes for, coiled everywhere?"

"Each has a special name and use. This one's to rescue Miss Day if she falls overboard. Tomorrow I'll show you the ropes if you want. Everything here is ropes. I even sleep in ropes," the sailor said.

Aoife looked up. "In the ropes? You'll fall into the sea."

"No, I mean... I'll show you tonight at eight bells when I come off watch."

"What are bells?"

"The day is divided into six, four-hour watches. Mid starts at Midnight. Morning at four AM. Forenoon at eight. Afternoon at noon. The Dog Watch is from 4 to 8 PM but split in two for our dinner break. I'm on the First Watch now until midnight. On each watch one bell is rung after a half hour, two after an hour, and so on until the end of the watch at 8 bells. So I'll see you at midnight, eight bells?"

"Sure, I guess, if I'm awake." Aoife was very sure she'd be listening for the bells.

Just then the captain called from the quarterdeck, "Carry on!" A nice breeze was stirring and the order was to hoist every bit of canvas the yardarms could carry. Their ship had three masts with three yards, or crosspieces each. So it meant "the whole nine yards."

Aoife thought he was referring to "carrying on" with the ladies because Faolan abruptly left her and scurried hand-over-fist up the ratlines (RAT-lins) of the mainmast. These were thin ropes tied between the vertical shrouds holding up the mast. There were sailors everywhere setting sails. They would stand on foot-ropes beneath the yards and lower the canvas by hand. Other sailors were pulling lines and singing sea shanties. The shantyman would sing the first line and the men would reply with the second. After a moment, Lemon came topside to play along with his fiddle and tap his long toes on the wooden deck.

When I was a little lad; And so my mother told me,
Way, haul away, we'll haul away, Joe!
That if I did not kiss the gals; Me lips would all grow mouldy.
Way, haul away, we'll haul away, Joe!

We squared our yards an' away we rolled, with the fiddles playin' handy,
Way, haul away, we'll haul away, Joe!
Wid a roll 'n' go, an' a westward ho, an' a Yankee Doodle Dandy.
Way, haul away, we'll haul away, Joe!

Way, haul away, the good ship is a-bolding,
Way, haul away, we'll haul away, Joe!
Way, haul away, the sheet is now unfolding,
Way, haul away, we'll haul away, Joe!

Then I got meself an Irish gal an' her name wuz
Flannigan,
  Way, haul away, we'll haul away, Joe!
She stole me boots, she stole me clothes, she
pinched me plate an' pannikin.
  Way haul away, we'll haul away Joe!

A hey can't you see the storm clouds are
gathering.

  Way, haul away, we'll haul for better weather,
    Way, haul away, we'll haul away, Joe!
  Way haul away, we'll haul away together,
    Way, haul away, we'll haul away, Joe!

The cook is in the galley boys; Making duff so
handy,
  Way, haul away, we'll haul away, Joe!
The captain's in his cabin lads; Drinking wine
and brandy,
  Way, haul away, we'll haul away, Joe!

  Way, haul away, I'll sing to you of Nancy,
    Way, haul away, we'll haul away, Joe!
  Way, haul away, she's just my cut and fancy,
    Way, haul away, we'll haul away, Joe!

There seemed to be a song for every task on the
ship and it was inspiring to see all the crew working
in unison. Not quite so with the Body of Christ,
thought Aoife. Romans 12:5. "*So it is with Christ's*
body. We are many parts of one body, and we all
belong to each other." She vowed never to argue
with Caitlín like she had with Saoirse. "Caitlín's
God is my God. Wherever she goes, I will go;
wherever she dies, I will die. We'll be good

Christian sisters to the end. Einin had said, '*To die is gain.*'"

When the men were done with the sails Faolan climbed a Jacob's ladder further up to the crow's-nest—really just a barrel strapped high on the mast. It swayed so much only experienced seamen could serve as lookouts. He didn't look down at her, so Aoife went below.

Aoife's Bible

It was time for Bible reading anyway and the girls were waiting.

"Caitlín and I were disagreeing," Bridget said. "She says there's a place called purgatory that burns off your small sins before you can go to heaven. I never heard of that in our Bible study."

"Go to 2nd Maccabees 12:39-46," said Caitlín.

"That's not in the Bible," said Aoife.

"Oh, I forgot some people don't use a whole Bible. Anyway, there was a battle. It says some Jews were collecting bodies of dead soldiers. When they found they were wearing small forbidden idols they prayed God would blot out this sin and let them into heaven. The book says it's a good thing to pray for the dead this way."

Bridget's eyes were squinting.

Aoife said, "We reject certain books because they contradict the rest of the Bible and, therefore, can't be from God."

Caitlín continued. "Well nevertheless, they weren't in hell, but couldn't be in heaven yet. That means there must be a place for saved dead people to be completely purified before entering holy heaven."

"You mean punished?" Bridget asked.

"Revelation 21:27 says nothing unclean shall enter heaven," Caitlín said.

Aoife looked it up:

27 Nothing evil will be allowed to enter, nor anyone who practices shameful idolatry and dishonesty—but only those whose names are written in the Lamb's Book of Life.

"What lamb is that?" Bridget asked.

"Jesus is the Lamb of God," Aoife said.

"*Agnus Dei,* in Latin," said Caitlín, "similar to the name of our ship according to Lemon."

"I thought the Lamb of God was slaughtered," said Bridget.

"I don't intend to be slaughtered in this ship," said Caitlín, "Holy Mary, Mother of God, pray for us sinners now and at the hour of our death." She looked away. "Aoife, please turn to 1st Corinthians 3:11-15."

For no one can lay any foundation other than the one we already have—Jesus Christ.

Anyone who builds on that foundation may use a variety of materials—gold, silver, jewels, wood, hay, or straw. But on the judgment day, fire will reveal what kind of work each builder has done. The fire will show if a person's work has any value. If the work survives, that builder will receive a reward. But if the work is burned up, the builder will suffer great loss. The builder will be saved, but like someone barely escaping through a wall of flames.

"I doubt any of us will die so holy we won't need purification to enter heaven," Caitlín said. "It can't be in heaven because of the fire, or in hell because we're already saved."

"Judgment," Aoife said, "refers to seeing if our works are good or bad. If good, we'll be rewarded; if bad, the loss is that we won't be able to please Jesus with them—and pleasing him is the very meaning of our existence."

Caitlín wrinkled her nose. "But people who do bad things still need to be punished," she said. "God is just."

"Wait," Bridget said. "When we die we go to be with Jesus right away because he already paid the price for our bad works and God doesn't see them at all."

Caitlín stared at her. "Bridget, you're being too simplistic."

Aoife held up her hand. "The truth is usually just that simple. When we die we're with Christ immediately. Like the thief on the cross next to Jesus. Luke 23:43, *'I assure you, today you will be with me in paradise.'* Also, there is Philippians 1:23, *'I'm torn between two desires: I long to go and be with Christ, which would be far better for me.'* And 2nd Corinthians 5:8, *'Yes, we are fully confident, and we would rather be away from these earthly bodies, for then we will be at home with the Lord.'* There's no mention of a purgatory."

Caitlín peered into Aoife's eyes. "Well, that sounds good enough for me, I suppose. I never wanted to go to purgatory anyway. I've got a humongous unconfessed sin and there's no priest on this ship."

Aoife took her hand and said, "1st Peter 2:5 tells us, *'And you are living stones that God is building into his spiritual temple. What's more, you are his holy priests. Through the mediation of Jesus*

Christ, you offer spiritual sacrifices that please God.' That means we are priests. We can go directly to God through Christ. Why don't you just confess your sin to me?"

"It's too awful. Later maybe," Caitlín said, glancing at Bridget.

Sleeping in Ropes

The girls settled into their bunks and Scannalan joined his little guardian. All was quiet except the gentle rolling of the ship and the moaning of its old boards. Aoife dozed off, mind wandering, dreaming about songs and sailors, but startled when she thought she heard seven bells, or was it eight? She peered into the darkness, but there was nary a candle flicker of fair Faolan—the one who had slipped a fish under her smock. Did he notice their hips had touched? Now they were going to America together to live on that farm by the brook. After laying still for half an hour she distinctly counted eight bells. They came in sets of two. She slipped away from Bridget and stood at the end of her bunk by Caitlín's feet. Soon a tiny glimmer could be seen descending, then a twinkle approaching. Presently it became a fire dancing on her, eventually developing the full beard and wild hair of her man, looming and putting a finger to his lips. The candle burned tall between them. Was it all in her head?

"Remember, I sleep hanging in ropes," he whispered dreamily, "did you wanna see?"

Aoife shook her head but followed his tiny light anyway. It's why she'd waited for the bells. He had to take her hand because of the dark and she felt a surge within her. She felt unworthy of such attention—being neither pretty nor precious. Yet the gem around her neck was both to her, and it gave her worth. She thought they'd be going topside, but instead he led her into his quarters. In darkness, every place seems like any other.

"Feel this," he whispered, guiding her hand over the rope hammock which was his bed.

"You sleep in this?" she murmured.

"The ship rocks me to sleep."

"You don't fall out?"

"No, it's easy. Wanna try it?"

Aoife shook her head again but attempted to lean on the edge rope. Nets are tricky, you can get caught in them—she was toppling over.

"Here," he said, catching her frail body and lifting it carefully in. She had no weight at all, like a fawn into a cradle. She gasped, but he put his fingers to her lips. She was embarrassed to be all skin and bones in his muscular arms. As the ropes embraced her some of her hair hung down through the mesh. Her pendant slid up to her chin. One slipper came off. She had never been carried by a man before and was certain it was sinful. Her insides told her so. Yet once in her life, before she died she deserved to be overwhelmed with such lovely feelings, didn't she? They pressed in on her like the weave of the hammock. She started to let go and relax into it. Her soul felt embraced. She couldn't believe what had just happened and where she was. All wrapped up. Then it was enough.

"I can't get out," she said, struggling. The hammock jerked violently.

"Here. Wait." He leaned over …

"Son of a gun, Aoife!" Caitlín barged in. "What do you think you're doing?"

This woke some of the other sailors and there ensued a general melee as the girls scurried out like mice from a closet.

"Nothing here shipmates," said Faolan, "Just dropped me candle. He picked up the slipper and stuffed it quickly into his shirt. Go back to sleep."

Outside the door Caitlín was furious. "Mary, Mother of God, Aoife! I woke up and you were gone. Bridget said you were in there, of all places. Does your God let you sin at will? Does he automatically forgive you from just any kind of behaviour?"

Aoife hung her head but didn't even try to flatten the smile on her face. She folded her arms across her rumpled frock. "We best get back to bed," she said. End of discussion. It was then she noticed she was wearing but one slipper.

Finally, they were resting quietly in their bunks.

"Caitlín."

"What? Shush. Go to sleep."

"Tomorrow we're both going in at eight bells."

"What?"

"Yeah, Faolan has a friend for you."

"What?"

"He saw you noticing him."

"Who? No!"

"Never mind, we'll discuss it in the morning. Go to sleep."

But Caitlín's eyes were full moons. Aoife's revenge felt sweet in her heart. But maybe she was dreaming the whole thing.

That morning when Bridget was up on deck, the girls were dressing behind their blanket. Caitlín was full and shapely. Aoife kidded, "One of these days you're gunna start to show, little Miss Innocence."

"Just leave that alone," said Caitlín, and her eyes meant it. "I'm not coddin' ya."

The Lay of the Land

Soon the *Agnes Dei* was ready to round the southern coast of Ireland and head directly west to America. Dead ahead was Fastnet Rock, a tiny teardrop in the sea and a sad farewell to the home country. There was no lighthouse yet on its tall 100-foot rocks, and at least one ship was soon destined to run aground with great loss of life. Aoife and Bridget were standing topside near the bowsprit when Lemon approached with his distinctive thump-thump-tap gait. He put his long arms around them like a mantis.

> 8
> So Poem Love did pluck a bone,
> From lonely Race's side;
> To mould a love for him to name;
> She was creation's pride.
> "Oh Wow," cried Race, "at last my flesh,"
> Her gloryshine grew bright.
> "I'll call her Racy!" he grabbed her tight;
> And hoped she'd spend the night.
> "She's bone in body, a copy of me,
> So I'll just call her Tracy.
> What name for her, describe or trace?
> She stays, I'll call her Stacy.
> But Love did grace her hair so lacy;
> I'm Race, she'll just be Grace."

Aoife replied:

God created skin,
Our blood, bones and hearts within—
Everything but sin.

Then gazing far out to sea, she began singing this hymn learned from her mom:

I sing the mighty power of God, that made the mountains rise,
That spread the flowing seas abroad, and built the lofty skies.
I sing the wisdom that ordained the sun to rule the day;
The moon shines full at his command, and all the stars obey.
I sing the goodness of the Lord, who filled the earth with food,
Who formed the creatures through the Word,
and then pronounced them good.
Lord, how Thy wonders are displayed, where'er I turn my eye,
If I survey the ground I tread, or gaze upon the sky.
There's not a plant or flower below,
but makes Thy glories known,
And clouds arise, and tempests blow, by order from Thy throne;
While all that borrows life from Thee is ever in Thy care;
And everywhere that we can be, Thou, God art present there.

"Did you write that, Effie?" asked Bridget.

"No she most certainly did not," said Lemon, "it was Isaac Watts—who also wrote 'Blest Is the Man Whose Bowels Move.'"

"Lemon! Go way outta that!" said Bridget. "Say, how come there's splashing white waves on only one side of that island?"

"Well, my wee Alanna, the wind is stiffening. It's blowing waves onto the left side of the island. See there? The other side is protected from the wind and has no waves. That's called the lee side of the island. The windward side is where the waves are."

88

"Which side will we go around?" Bridget asked.

"You have to know the 'lay of the land.' If the land is flat and sandy, the seabed is likely to be the same. In this case, it's steep and rocky. One side is more dangerous than the other. A ship sailing along an island's windward shore with land on the ship's lee side (away from the wind) could get blown onto the rocks. That makes it a lee shore relative to the boat. Always shape up your course to avoid a lee shore. If you get too close you might not be able to claw away. On the other side of the island, the wind would just blow you further out to sea and save you from sinking. "

"How come you know so much?" Bridget asked. "And oh, if we get killed in a shipwreck is there a purgatory or not?"

"Well, I believe it's either heaven or hell for us. But hell is too final a thing for a loving God. So you can get out of hell if you've been punished enough and God shows mercy. You never know. It's all in his sovereign hands. On Judgment Day, the dead will be raised to give an account of how they lived—good deeds weighed against the bad. If in the end, the good are heavier they will go to heaven. But first they must give some of their good works to those they offended in this life. If their good deeds are all used up in making up for wrongs they did to others, then the offended get to give them some of their own bad deeds. So the person ends up suffering in hell for many people's wrongs.

Matthew 25:29 says, "*To those who use well what they are given, even more will be given, and they will have an abundance. But from those who do nothing, even what little they have will be taken away."*

This logic didn't sit right with the girls. But there it was, right in the Bible. Or was it?

The University

Father Jean Marie Delacroix wore his clerical robes to class at Université Laval Faculté de Médecine in Québec City. They lent him an air of billowing dignity. Soon he discovered that white lab coats or scrub gowns could have the same effect. And he loved parading before patients and parishioners alike. He could pull this off because of his excellence in academics and friendly, if superior manner with all people.

He thought his life happy and fulfilled. It was not, however, without issues with the teaching being received. The most common procedure in hospital was bloodletting. He learned to "breathe a vein" by drawing blood from one or more of the larger external vessels in the forearm or neck. He used a scalpel or a brass box with sharp steel blades, called a "scarificator." This had a spring-loaded mechanism with gears that snapped several blades out, then in through slits in the front cover. Not unlike some instruments of torture. Leeches could also be used; there were jars and jars of them in the cabinet. These suckers brought with them their own anticoagulant. Bloodletting was used to treat almost

90

every sort of human "ailment," including nosebleeds and childbirth. Before amputation, it was customary to remove a quantity of blood equal to the amount believed to circulate in that limb. The process was usually continued until the patient began to faint.

The rationale for bloodletting was that it was necessary to keep bodily fluids, or "humours" in proper balance to maintain health. No one could tell him just what this balance might be. The ancient practice was remaining popular because any kind of treatment seemed better than none at all, and at any rate, it made the patients feel like something was being done for them.

Meanwhile the underlying causes of disease remained elusive. Jean had his opinions about this and something inside him hinted that bloodletting was wrong. He recalled Leviticus 17:14. *The life of every creature is in its blood...* Maybe that was significant.

Still perhaps breathing a vein once in a while was better than any of the useless and dangerous elixirs, tonics, and potions sitting on the shelf next to the leeches.

Chapter 5

Co talla forum, ré n-dul it láma,
mo chuit, mo chotlud, ar méit do gráda.
Rop tussu t' áenur m' urrann úais amra:
ní chuinngim daíne ná maíne marba.

Till I am able to pass into thy hands,
My treasure,
my beloved through the greatness of thy love
Be thou alone my noble and wondrous estate.
I seek not men nor lifeless wealth.

Troubled Waters

God, you hound my back;
Where can I flee your love cross?
How deep runs the sea?

Caulking on the old ship deck-boards had
become loose over years of constant motion—even
to the point of gapping. Not that they would catch a
toe, but Bridget was sitting by Caitlín's bunk one
day when the ship changed tack. She felt a sharp
pinch on her bottom and when she tried to rise
found that *Agnes* had grabbed her dress.

"Caitlín, I can't get up."

"You're kidding."

"Ask me arse!" Bridget was pulling at the cloth.

"Well, get out of that frock, silly, before you tear it." They were both laughing.

"Okay… okay, now what? Do I prance about in the nip all day?"

Just then Lemon happened by. "Alanna my dear, I was going to invite you for a stroll on deck, but that might prove breezy in such garb."

Caitlín started rummaging through Bridget's burlap sack.

"It's the only clothes I got," the little waif announced, grabbing her blanket and marching off with Lemon—a tiny banshee with a tall wizard. Aoife tumbled off her bunk and trundled after them. Bridget said, "Let's walk all the way to the back of the ship." She adjusted her blanket, being careful the fresh breezes didn't flirt too playfully with its corners. It took them several minutes to walk the deck. The ocean was frisky and they were still developing sea legs.

"The rear is called the stern," Lemon said, "or 'la poupe' in French. That's why we're standing on the poop deck."

"I thought it was where the Captain's loo was."

"Oh don't be stupid, Biddy," said Aoife, giving her a playful shove, harder than she meant to.

Bridget clenched her fists. "Not as stupid as you talking and playing smiley all the time with a sailor."

"Oh my word," said Lemon, turning on Aoife, "you know of course, that necklace of yours has aphrodisiac powers. Maybe we ought to take it off you and put it on poor Alanna here—where it's not likely to have any such effect."

"I would love to have afro-delic powers," Bridget said, reaching out for Aoife's neck.

Aoife covered her front with both hands and glared at Lemon. "Don't. It makes me feel precious and worthy." She spun away and swept below decks to be with Caitlín.

"Never mind Aoife," said Lemon, "she's just making an idol out of a stone, I'm afraid. Whatever sweetens her tea. By the way, do you know your name means 'little chick?'"

"I thought 'biddy' meant an annoying granny."

"Well that too, but also you, especially dressed up in that fuzzy blanket with your cute beak of a nose. Would you like to see where I live?"

"Oh yes," Bridget chirped, shrugging her shoulders, "is there steerage back here too?"

"Well no, but originally it referred to the area closest to the rudder. Now it means anywhere the cheapest bunks are. But I have a cabin right next to Captain Mack's."

"Wow," Bridget said when they opened the door to the tiny room. There was a proper bed with sheets, a small dressing table, and even a tiny glass porthole with brass rim. Everything was clean and painted white. "How do you rate this?"

"How do you think?" said Lemon, jingling his pouch of lucky charms. It seemed to Bridget that it was fat as ever.

"Can I have one of those, please Mister Lemon?"

Lemon stroked his beard. "You only get one so keep it safe and spend it wisely."

She clasped it tightly in both hands. When they got back to their bunks the ship had gone over to another tack. Bridget shed her blanket and retrieved her dress from the grip of the planking. Then she placed her only precious possession into the only pocket she had ever owned.

The Attack

Meanwhile, Aoife and Caitlín had gone deep into the hold. They sat among the wooden boxes and barrels strapped to the hull. Caitlín was crying.

"My Aunt Astrid's such an old biddy," she said. "Yeah, so what if I was toying with someone that day, and dancing with his eyes? I'm old enough. I was enjoying his hand in my hair and then pressing on my back. He called me his flower. I tingled when he pulled me near himself. What's wrong with tingling? I felt protected and not rejected for once. Not judged. Precious. He was being sweet and tender. We just wanted to be— enfolded—as rose petals. Hungered for it—you know what I mean?"

Aoife stared at her blankly—what did Caitlín know about hunger? And what did Aoife know about rose petals?

"There was something wrong with our breathing. I told him to stop; I told *me* to stop. But we wouldn't; I mean *he* wouldn't. I was going under and tried to scream. Maybe I did—I must have. He was stealing something from me."

"It's not a sin to be raped," Aoife said.

"It is, when your body responds," Caitlín said. "When it feels pleasure. *That*—you can never wash away in the shower. God, I wish I had teeth down there instead of lips. That's my sin. I joined into my own attack. And now, that sin endures—is growing inside me as a cancer."

"1st John 1:9," Aoife said, "*But if we confess our sins to him, he is faithful and just to forgive us our sins and to cleanse us from all wickedness.*"

"Forgiveness? Get real! My parents threw me out of the house. It was either Our Lady Magdalene Convent Laundry or my awful 'Aunt Acid' in Dungrath. Aoife, *if your eye causes you to sin, gouge it out*, I can't mother a monster, conceived in sin—feeding off my flesh. I won't. It would be an unpardonable sin to live with such an evil growing inside me. God is going to cleanse me from this wickedness."

"But…" Aoife tried to hug her but she shied away.

"Don't mock my grief unless you can embrace it. I need you on my side. I stole her gold and jewellery and I'm running away on this ship. Are you with me or against me?"

"I will walk by your side, my sister. Just don't go where I can't follow."

Caitlín broke down and sobbed on her shoulder.

The girls grasped each other, swayed by the rhythmic rocking of the ship—and the mounting break of waves on its sides. The planks moaned and Aoife joined them, "*Where you go, I will go; where you lodge, I will lodge.*" She knew very well what that would mean. Everything had got quite twisted and turned backwards.

The Funeral

The first death came a few hours later—an old man too weak to travel in the first place. But a father and grandfather nevertheless. Thin with dysentery, his dead blue lips still reflecting his pain.

Aoife closed his eyelids with gentle fingers and combed his thin silvery hair. In the workhouse, the girls had learned to prepare bodies for burial, but the ship had no supplies. Aoife's mind dragged her screaming back to Blarnybrae—she felt again like God's insidious instrument of death. Reaping nothing but wrath. "Oh cruel God. Why use my hand for this vile work?"

Nevertheless, she washed the poor gentleman with a bucket of seawater to remove any pollution and dressed him in his best clothes. Next, they tied some rusty chain around his ankles and wrapped him in a bit of old torn sail canvas. Faolan stitched it up into a shroud.

"Be sure to set the last stitch through his nose," Lemon said.

"Why on God's great green earth would..." Bridget recoiled from the spectacle.

"Says to in the prayer book," Lemon said, "if he ain't quite dead he'll wake fast enough. Also, keeps his ghost from getting out."

"Aragh! If yous did that to me I'd haunt yous for sure. So why the chain?"

"It's a sinker to keep his ghost from surfacing and haunting us," Lemon said.

After this they draped a Union Jack over him and in a short but solemn procession carried him to the lee gangway for the sea burial. The ship was stopped and the yards cockbilled, some tilted up, others down in salute. The bosun ordered: "Ship's Company ---- OFF Hats."

There was no chaplain on board so the captain, who had dutifully ascertained that the deceased was neither unbaptized, nor excommunicate, nor had committed suicide, then read from Aoife's Bible:

He said,
"I came naked from my mother's womb,
and I will be naked when I leave.
The Lord gave me what I had,
and the Lord has taken it away.
Praise the name of the Lord!"

Job 1:21

After all, we brought nothing with us when we came
into the world, and we can't take anything with us
when we leave it.

1st Timothy 6:7

"But as for me, I know that my Redeemer lives,
and he will stand upon the earth at last.
And after my body has decayed,
yet in my body I will see God!
I will see him for myself.
Yes, I will see him with my own eyes.
I am overwhelmed at the thought!

Job 19:25-27

Jesus told her, "I am the resurrection and the
life. Anyone who believes in me will live, even after
dying. Everyone who lives in me and believes in me
will never ever die. Do you believe this, Martha?"

John 11:25-26

Psalm 39:4, 5
"Lord, remind me how brief my time on earth will
be.
Remind me that my days are numbered—
how fleeting my life is.
You have made my life no longer than the width of
my hand.
My entire lifetime is just a moment to you;
at best, each of us is but a breath."

1st Corinthians 15:43-44
Our bodies are buried in brokenness, but they will
be raised in glory. They are buried in weakness, but
they will be raised in strength. They are buried as
natural human bodies, but they will be raised as
spiritual bodies. For just as there are natural
bodies, there are also spiritual bodies.

Then the captain read from the 1662 edition of
the Book of Common Prayer:

Forasmuch as it hath pleased Almighty God of
his great mercy to take unto himself the soul of our
dear brother here departed: we therefore commit
his body to the Deep, to be turned into corruption,
looking for the resurrection of the body, (when the
sea shall give up her dead,) and the life of the world
to come, through our Lord Jesus Christ; who at his
coming shall change our vile body, that it may be
like his glorious body, according to the mighty
working, whereby he is able to subdue all things to
himself.

The sailors then tilted the board that held the
body which slid feet first from under the flag.
Weighted as it was, it sank swiftly into the sea.

Directly after this, the bosun called "Ship's
Company ---- Dismissed Hats!" and the captain
ordered the ship to get under way again.

The Storm

After that, Aoife and Caitlín went down into the hold for one of their private talks.

"What am I going to do about…?"

"I'll take care of it," Aoife said, "simply trust me." She wondered if committing a sin for the good of another person would be entirely bad. Caitlín's eyes looked so reassured and peaceful.

Just then, they were interrupted by several sailors scurrying about the girls' knees looking for ropes and other gear. "Get back to your bunks, yous beef-witted wenches," they said. "We're battening down the hatches."

"What?"

"Storm's coming," said Caitlín. "Battens are long, flat wooden blades which keep the tarpaulins in place. —So you'll help me then?"

"I said I've got you covered," whispered Aoife, pulling her up. "Soon, my dear. Don't fear the coming storm."

They parted and Aoife made her way across the lower decks to Lemon's cabin. She was greeted with this:

9
The Spirit Song of note and rest,
Saw Grace did satisfy;
So fit the two in deep deep love,
"Be fruitful and multiply."
But later Glare found Grace a Feed,
Red ripe, but quite unfit;
"But Love said don't eat this," she said,
"Or even be licking it."
"No! Poem Love spits lies," said Glare;
"Go surely bite and chew.

Or bake a better pie than Poem's own;
You'll be smarter if you do."
So Grace did suck that one taboo,
And Race showed no backbone.

"Are you getting seasick?" Lemon asked.

"No," said Aoife, "but I need you to cast a spell on Caitlín so she'll abort her rape child."

Lemon gaped at her wide-eyed. "I didn't even know she was with squirrel. If you're really serious, I'm afraid you're out of luck. In such cases I usually prescribe 'Farrer's Catholic Pills,' but I left all my supplies behind. Before that, I used an emulsion of crushed ants, camel saliva, and deer tail hairs, simmered in bear fat. All in short supply here. Sorry."

Romans 12:12

**Violence in prayer,
Flowing frantic tears at God—
Joy now losing Hope.**

"But she's desperate, she says it's like an albatross hung around her neck. I fear she might harm herself with the water ladle handle."

Lemon shuddered for a moment and closed his eyes. "Albatross do not fly over this ocean. I do have a supply of Spanish Fly to sell to sailors in port. I grind up emerald-green blister beetles. Ingested it irritates the organs resulting in increased blood flow that mimics excitement in men. It's a popular, but dangerous aphrodisiac. In increased doses it can be an abortifacient for the ladies."

Aoife blanched. It seemed unnatural and grotesque to her. "Give me all of it," she said, level-eyed.

"Well no," Lemon stroked his beard, "be careful; too much is fatal."

The storm mounted up gradually and the first day was just a time of rocking in bunks. Lemon came to visit the girls in the evening. "Are yous under the weather yet?" This expression came from boat passengers who would go below decks or "under the weather" where the rolling of the ship was less.

"Not me," Bridget bragged, "but a bunch of the others are puking. Caitlín for instance. The ship is swinging too much."

"Ships don't swing," said Lemon. "They have six motions. The *roll* is leaning to port, then to starboard; the *pitch* is seesawing bow to stern; *yaw* is a spinning motion; *surge* is being pushed forward; *sway* is sideways; and **heave** is an upward…"

Bridget cut him off with a gulp, racing madly for the toilet below.

Lemon gave Caitlín a compassionate smile. To Aoife on the bunk above, he gave a small paper packet of what looked like green dust. It was sealed with the red wax <L^oL> imprint of his signet ring. "Only a pinch mind you," he said, "with water."

Aoife took a tin cup to the scuttlebutt and filled it a quarter full. When she got back Lemon was gone. She tapped in a small amount of powder and swished it around in the cup. She tapped again for good measure till it looked like green tea, which she fed sideways to a groggy Caitlín, already green around the gills.

"I know another motion of ships," Bridget said, returning. "*Sinking!*" She flopped down beside Caitlín, too exhausted to climb up to her sister. "What was that she gave you?"

"Just water," Aoife interrupted.

"Then what's in that little envelope?" Bridget grabbed it, spilling some.

"Why, this looks like Lemon's Spanish Fly."

"Did he tell you about that?"

"I look through all his things," said Bridget. "He said it's for sailors to 'dab it up with dollymops.' So why's Caitlín having it? She's already got a bun in the oven."

Aoife raised an eyebrow at her sister. She was a little sponge, absorbing fair and foul alike. Older than she appeared, perhaps. Growing unnaturally fast? Maybe she'd have been better off back in her cottage on the green hills, protected from the vulgar outside world. "How'd you know she is with child?" Aoife asked.

"Lemon told me; he tells me everything."

Aoife looked at her sternly. "Well, for very good reasons, we need to take this bun out of the oven."

"I think it's a crime to waste food," Bridget said. "I wouldn't want my insides to become a crime scene. I wouldn't want my tummy to become a tomb."

At daybreak, there was a piercing, high-pitched sound. The deck crew foreman, or 'boatswain' (BO-sun) was in charge of just about everything from the gunwales down. He had an annoying shrill whistle which emitted different notes for every occasion from *mess call* to *swab the deck* time. Aoife was sure they were all designed to wake sleeping passengers. Now he was piping a new bosun's call: *all hands on deck*. There were special tasks to prepare for a storm. The sailors scurried about like ants in rain. There were knots to be tied, canvas to be rolled or unrolled, ropes to be stretched or coiled. After about an hour came *pipe down*, which dismissed all crew not on watch. The bosun was always calling for something, it seemed.

"How do we get him to pipe down?" Bridget complained. But nobody could hear her.

A terrible rain was pelting the deck above them. Aoife opened the hatch but the wind drove her back. She did catch a glimpse of two sailors wrestling with a thrashing sheet, trying to tie down the corner of a sail. They were just apparitions—sailcloth oilskins sloshing over black gumboots, topped with broad-brimmed Sou'westers. The sky's angry veins throbbed with lightning amidst thunderous bellows. The ship, but a speck in the ocean, was reduced to bare poles leaning dangerously near the swirling froth. Her stern heaved and struggled to climb swell after mountainous swell as she was driven before the wind, shot from some giant bow. Each time, her bow would bow to bite the wave just passed. Faolan was at the helm fighting to keep her from yawing and being swamped by a wave over the side.

Aoife wiped her face; saltwater stung her eyes, her nose, and ran down her throat. She'd inhaled sea spray. "It's deadly out there," she sputtered. The wind in mad cacophony was playing the rigging like cello strings and the masts as bassoon reeds. Whitecaps were beating rhythm insanely against the hull.

Tossed on seas of storm,
Fear not! I know the captain;
We're safe; he's my dad.

But spiritually, Aoife felt beaten up. As for God, she became unsure about what she knew was certain. Surely these poor souls around her didn't deserve the wrath they were experiencing—wrath beyond human endurance—wrath unto death. She was being *tossed here and there by waves and carried about by every wind of doctrine.*" Ephesians 4:11-14 (NASB). And little wonder, for she had no mother church to build her up in understanding as a mature believer.

The wind and waves lasted all day, and then another. Many of the passengers became incapacitated, so Captain McCrawly assigned Aoife, Faolan, and Lenna Ó Leannáin to section off an infirmary of sorts amidships. Caitlín was the first to occupy a bunk. Aoife decided to move there to be near her.

"I'm coming too then," Bridget said, "I don't want to be left alone here on me tot."

"Then you'll have to help with nursing duties."

"I can do it, so long as I don't toss my cookies over everything."

Sickbay filled up fast and they had to expand it twice. The storm would surge and ebb but never surrendered. They had to use rolled up blankets and rope to prevent sick bodies from spilling onto the deck. Life was becoming a fight for existence, with nature ever wrestling for the ultimate death grip.

"The wretched people are too weak to vomit," Bridget said, "and there's nothing in their bodies anyway."

Then Caitlín became very ill, but not from seasickness alone.

Psalm 139
*13 You made all the delicate, inner parts of my body
and knit me together in my mother's womb.
14 Thank you for making me so wonderfully complex!
Your workmanship is marvelous—how well I know it.
15 You watched me as I was being formed in utter seclusion,
as I was woven together in the dark of the womb.
16 You saw me before I was born.
Every day of my life was recorded in your book.
Every moment was laid out
before a single day had passed.*

"And then I was passed—a ruddy human discharge the size of a sparrow but with my living fingers and toes. My tiny nose. My smile. Innocent, yet poisoned and expelled as an irritant, I left my dying epitaph, my accusation in red on the white sheets. My mother seemed callous, oblivious; it was Biddy who found me bloody between her legs, wrapped me carefully in a handkerchief, and laid me in a tin soup bowl on the heaving table."

"Get rid of that," said Aoife, brushing by.

"Where?"

"Down the toilet."

"What? This is a child of God," said Bridget, "I can't fathom how one sin makes another okay."

"You're being too simplistic," said Aoife.

"Psalm 127 says children are a gift from the Lord..." Bridget's voice trailed off; Aoife was busying herself with three other bodies.

106

Bridget scooped up the bowl and without putting on weather gear of any kind, climbed out on deck and reverently poured its contents into the sea. Rain dripped through her hair and mingled with tears. "May this be a bowl of salvation, not judgement. I christen thee Muirín (MIR-een), meaning 'born of the sea,' and commit thee to thy maker who is all good and caring for his every sparrow."

Then she said:

> *"Christ alone: You're my keel, my mast;*
> *What wave can break, what storm can blast?*
> *My sails are strong, my rudder true;*
> *My anchor holds, my love is You.*
>
> *When darkness overwhelms my gaze,*
> *Your Spirit song bursts forth in praise;*
> *May my last breath, of this present race,*
> *Speak not of me, but of Your grace."*

Dripping wet, she struggled below, stripped and slipped into her bunk to be alone for a while.

That night there were two more deaths from diarrhoea and dehydration. Next morning, due to the storm, the crew struggled to haul them topside and irreverently dumped them over the side. No chain, no shroud, no stitching, no ceremony.

No one had thought of Scannalan since the storm began. Terrified, the first day he hid in the hold among the water barrels. When he tried to return to Bridget he discovered she had moved, so he set out in search. He knew he had to tread gingerly to avoid the captain who was afraid he carried disease, the bosun who wanted him for the stirabout, and most of the older women who still considered him a rat. Actually, the rodent population was dwindling nicely because of him. Finally, he came across not Bridget but his old master, Lenna Ó Leannáin who greeted him with open arms and a tall, steady shoulder to ride on. He felt calm in the storm, snuggling next to the long grey beard. Lemon carried him about proudly and shielded him from menacing hands, if not the stares. Truth be known, the old man rather enjoyed flaunting him in front of everyone. They did make a peculiar pair indeed.

The storm lingered on for days—unnaturally so. Some of the sailors began grumbling to the bosun about Lemon.

"He's a canvas short of full sail," they said, "and what be his int'rest in those girls and wild beasts? S'not natural. And where does he get his barmbrack bread from? With jam every morning."

"He's just an eccentric old salt," the bosun said, fingering the lucky charm in his pocket.

"Nay, we're of a mind he's the Jonah responsible for this weather."

"Be that as it may, there's nothing we can do about it."

"We can toss him overboard, we can. Like it says in the Bible. Him and that bewitched cat of his."

In spite of the bosun's protest, the mob dragged Lemon on deck and prepared to throw him over. Scannalan bared his teeth and hissed at them.

"If I have caused this storm then I can calm it," Lemon said, wrenching free from their grip. With this, he reached into his bag and drew out three green wafers. "Waters, I rebuke thee in the name of the Father, the Son, and the Holy Dove." With each name, he tossed in one charm. At the third, all the chop on the sea vanished. There were no whitecaps or plumes of salt spray anywhere. The wind ceased and the sun broke out. Everyone was amazed at the power displayed, and drew back from Lemon. He quickly and calmly retreated below deck.

The waves then appeared to have glassy sides and the sun shone through them a beautiful transparent blue. It was mesmerizing to watch them rise and fall, to see them grow even stronger, ever taller until the ship was being lifted dangerously high into the air. With no wind to push her, she yawed sideways and helplessly slipped down the face of each wave. In the troughs, the swells became walls like some great parted sea; higher they grew. Lemon was hastily summoned again. This time, Bridget and the captain accompanied him.

"Is this what you call calming the storm?" the captain demanded.

Lemon, confused, threw in three more charms, then six more. Still the waves grew. Terrified, everyone retreated below like prairie dogs.

Everyone but Bridget that is. She held tight, standing on a box, chin resting on the gunwale until well into night. Then with knuckles white, and knees trembling she breathed, "Oh Father, forgive me for not praying until now. Forgive me for doubting you are the Most High King over even waves and storms. Forgive me for not making you Lord over all of me, all of the time. I ask only that you might soothe the heart of this storm beast and that you might bring small Muirín unto yourself. She is now lost at sea—like us all." It became as if some great Spirit was praying for her.

Nothing happened, so she struggled below. But it was *a night of watching* by the Lord. (Exodus 12:42)

The next day the storm had abated and the ship was running fast before favourable breezes. The deck had dried out. Lenna Ó Leannáin and Bridget emerged from a hatch for one of their walks. The sailors greeted him warmly but Scannalan bared his teeth nevertheless. The men thanked him for calming the storm and secretly hoped he would bestow on them other miracles as well. "Curious," thought Lemon, who knew very well it was *the finger of God* (Exodus 8:19), not his Connemara marble wafers. Bridget just smiled and remained silent.

They gazed peacefully across the wake of the ship and the flattened waters. After a few minutes, Lemon pointed out a tiny triangular fin jutting from the water, trailing the ship.

"That must be a whale of a shark," he said, "to be seen from this distance."

"Why would a whale follow us?" Bridget asked.

"No—shark. For food scraps thrown overboard, I presume," said Lemon. "Certainly not for sport like dolphins. Sharks are coldblooded killers and eat anything. Still in the womb, their unborn pups will battle and consume each other, and even any unfertilized eggs they can find. All the earth is cursed."

Bad News

When Bridget returned to her bunk Caitlín seemed to be better.

"The storm has died," Caitlín said, "did you say a prayer?"

Aoife butt in, "We don't 'say' prayers; we just talk to God."

"Well, that's what I meant," Caitlín said, giving her a look.

Just then Scannalan scampered over across the floor. He could freely roam the ship now, being under the protection of Lemon. He jumped in to snuggle with Caitlín, who turned up her nose, but put an arm around him anyway.

Aoife opened her Bible.

Bígí láidir agus bíodh misneach mhór agaibh, ná himeaglaígí, agus ná bíodh uamhan agaibh rompu: óir is é do Thiarna Dia a théid libh; ní fheallfaidh sé ort agus ní threigfidh sé thú.

So be strong and courageous! Do not be afraid and do not panic before them. For the Lord your God will personally go ahead of you. He will neither fail you nor abandon you.
Deuteronomy 31:6

Her big eyes rose from the page. "It's not about the storm. I've some bad news for us all. Some of the patients in our little sickbay have more than seasickness and dysentery. They're developing rashes and fevers. We need to … well, I guess just keep them as clean and comfortable as possible. There's no medicine on board for this."

Bridget approached a small boy lying with his sleeping mother. He was cradled protectively in her arms. "How do you feel? How can I help?"

"My headache and I'm so cold," he said, trembling.

Bridget pulled a blanket over him.

"And my mother ain't moving no more."

Bridget felt her forehead. She was cold as the air around them—her eyes wide, fixed on the heavy beam just above. The girl quickly closed them with tender fingertips and slipped her limp son from under her rigour stiff arms. He was light as a dead evergreen sprig. "You'll be more comfortable over here. We'll take care of your dear mum."

When she returned, Bridget noticed the mother was wearing a gold necklace. Naturally the emigrants would bring whatever valuables they might have. "No purpose in dumping that into the sea," Bridget thought, so she clasped it around her own neck, intending to save it for the boy. But after just hours the boy joined his mother in the ocean and Bridget wondered what to do about the jewellery. There were no relatives she knew of. Why should Lemon or the captain pocket it? It wasn't theirs. And Aoife already had her necklace. So she decided to keep it hidden safe and see what might happen.

And the shark trailed relentlessly after them.

The next day, the lookout spotted a clipper ship approaching dead ahead, carrying passengers from Baltimore to Cork and then on to Liverpool. Faolan went below to fetch Aoife and they stood together at the bowsprit gunwale, her hair blowing in his face.

"You look radiant this morning," he remarked through the fine strands.

"You must be joking," she replied, "that ship is the only beauty here."

"Yes indeed," the boy agreed a bit too readily, "see how she sails along at a good clip, a real lovely." As it passed he added. "Much faster than us. She carries more sails; see the skysails on three masts and the moonrakers even higher." He pointed with his whole arm. "Look, studdingsails on booms jutting out from the hull. It's all about speed. In storms, we have to shorten sail. But she plows on, heeling over so much her lee rails dip the water."

"Exciting," Aoife said, her breath visible in misty puffs.

A clipper ship is too fine-lined a girl to carry much cargo but this one did have a good lot of spuds on board—to feed the passengers and also to sell as seed potatoes. Unknown to everyone, each tuber carried a cargo of its own: the blight *Phytophthora infestans*, which originated in North America and spread to all of Europe. It carried death to more than potatoes.

"Do you wish you were on that one, heading home?" Faolan asked. "Not that she'd bother to stop for a gam with us."

"Actually, I'm right where I wanna be," Aoife hinted, nudging him with her bony shoulder. "When we get to America are you going to sail back on this ship?"

"No," he said, staring out at the receding clipper, "I've a mind to find me a sturdy, full-bodied pioneer woman and head out west to Iowa Territory with our baby."

Aoife's thin frame shuddered, so the boy took her elbow and helped her below. They didn't speak.

There was a hovering smell of rotting flesh and Bridget had prepared four more bodies to bring up.

The shark trailed on.

Lemon was treating gangrenous toes with fly maggots. "They only eat the dead flesh," he said. Nevertheless, the odour was sickening and the sight of them writhing in wounds, ghastly.

"Would you rather have maggots, or start doing amputations?" he asked Aoife.

"They're all dying anyway," she said, "damn the rats to hell."

"Not all, we pray," he said. "Typhus is transmitted by fleas which jump from the rats to humans. When they bite people they spread the bacteria *Rickettsia prowazekii*, which grow in louse tummies and are pooped in their faeces. The disease is then transmitted to an uninfected person who scratches the itchy louse bite and rubs the excrement into the wound."

"Yuck," was all Aoife had to say; she was tired of his endless technical descriptions about everything. So Lemon tried to change the mood with his poem:

> 10
> Their gloryshine blinked off and died;
> The nakedness was stark;
> They hid from Poem Love in leaves,
> And waited for the dark.
> So Love must curse the spinning world,
> For Race became a sinner:
> The Feed grew stubborn, Pets ran wild,
> And ate each other for dinner.
> Now Grace knew pain in having young,
> And longed to be the boss,
> Then Glare from dust bit her son's heel,

But Glare's head is applesauce.
It happened on a wooden cross,
And a resurrection that is real.

Aoife was weary of the death around her. She was sick of everything. She groped blindly about her business, doing most of the nursing and cleaning. "Lord, I'm getting more miserable every day," she prayed, "but I know that's very sinful, as I ought to put my trust in You, who afflicteth not willingly. Are trials sent to try my faith? O may I not despair, but may my faith become ever stronger."

I've been in backpace.
And before His constant grace,
I fall on my face.

Except for bringing more maggots and pulling the odd tooth with a pair of medieval-looking pliers, Lemon mostly stayed in his aft cabin. He did institute the custom of "conclamation" on board. To make sure a person was really dead they would all gather around and yell their name three times. If there was no reaction the patient was assumed departed. No doubt there must have been a few tossed overboard alive.

Lemon just stared down into his candle, breathing the warm air over it, trying not to become infected. Death was winning the battle. For his part, Scannalan ate as many rats as he could, but was able to do only so much against so many.

Bridget was the one who prayed with the dying, held their hands, and prepared them for mortality and burial at sea. The latest was a young boy who had just lost two parents, and three toes to gangrene.

116

He looked pale and languid lying surrendered in his straw. Like Bridget, he had wild hair like hay but a sweet face with large, moist eyes.

"What's your name, gentle boy?"

"I'm Kevin," he told the nice girl, coughing. The hatch above them was open and the sun shone brilliantly behind her head. "Are you my angel of light?" he mumbled, shielding his eyes. "You're much too bright, way too beautiful! It hurts to look at you. Please hasten me to the Lord."

Bridget had borrowed Aoife's Bible, which her sister didn't appear to have much time for anymore.

Coimhéadaigí sibh féin i ngrá Dé, ag súil le trocaire ár dTiarna Íosa Críost, chun na beatha marthanaí.

… she read to the boy and he closed his eyes.

Jude 21: *"and await the mercy of our Lord Jesus Christ, who will bring you eternal life. In this way, you will keep yourselves safe in God's love."*

To pass the time they counted to a hundred, then backwards, and recited the alphabet together: A, B, C… W, X, Y, and Z and *per se* AND. Yes, back then there were 27 letters. "*Per se*" means "by itself," so "&" stood as a letter by itself. Bridget read it from some old books she found in the captain's cabin: The New England Primer and the Dixie Primer. Over time, "and *per se* AND" became shortened to "ampersand."

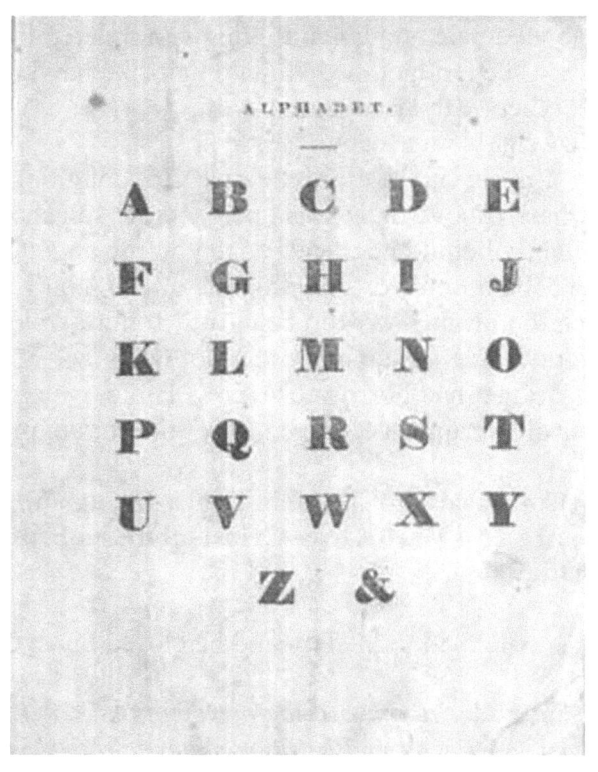

She stared into his big eyes and read:

94. Now I lay me down to sleep,
I pray Thee, Lord, my soul to keep ;
If I should die before I wake,
I pray Thee, Lord, my soul to take.

And this on the next page:

Jesus, Saviour, pity me,
Hear me when I cry to Thee ;
I've a very wicked heart,
Full of sin in ev'ry part.

I can never make it good ;
Wilt Thou wash me in Thy blood ?
Jesus, Saviour, pity me,
Hear me when I pray to Thee.

When I try to do Thy will,
Sin is in my bosom still,
And I soon do something bad ;
Then my heart is dark and sad.

Now I come to Thee for aid,
All my hope on Thee is stayed ;
Thou hast bled and died for me,
I will give myself to Thee.

"Little boy," Bridget asked. "Do you have a wicked heart?"

"Oh you know I do," he replied. "I need Jesus more than anything."

"Then I give Him to you," said the girl, "I already have Him. But my heart has always been good, not wicked. I have never denied Him. And never will."

She continued reading:

An-na Mood was a good child.
She said her prayers each day.
She loved God, and tried to do all He told her
*   in His word.*
So God took her home to live with Him.
She died and went to Heaven.
Do you not wish to be like An-na ?

"I love you, my An-na an-gel," the boy spoke. "Mother gave me this just before she... Would you wear my ring? Would you be my true and faithful bride until death do us part?"

Bridget blushed and bowed her head. She put a hand to his forehead and withdrew it immediately.

"Oh dear," he said, "I'm thinking I'll be needing your answer real soon." With this, he slipped the diamond on her finger and held the hand tightly. She bent down and kissed his cheek.

"Poor hot boy, I'd be honoured to wear your ring forever," she whispered into his ear, giving him a hug that lasted tight until the end.

Drained, she made her way on deck where she could cry into the wind—and vomit down the side of the ship. She did not feel safe in God's love at all. She'd long since abandoned any hope of escape from the contagion. Now she had actually lain alongside one of them to share his death. But "*Yea, though I walk through the valley of the shadow of death, I will fear no evil: for thou art with me; thy rod and thy staff they comfort me.*" Psalm 23:4. She tried her best to believe, but the Lord had to help her.

Still the shark trailed on.

Yet God was indeed watching and comforting as she did His work. She was not coming down with Typhus and even her seasickness was subsiding. Because of her kindness, many were giving her their necklaces, rings, and brooches. The men had wedding bands and gold coins for her. She accumulated so much precious loot she took to stashing it in the bottom of her burlap sack. She told no one, not even Aoife. It was nobody's business but her own. She was quickly becoming the wealthiest person on the ship.

A New Birth

They had been sailing for almost a month with 30 deaths and one birth. That little girl came in the wee hours of the night with very little crying. Bridget snatched her away when she found her between a dead mother's legs.

Meanwhile Aoife, unable to sleep, had joined Faolan on his watch. They stared together at an eerie white bioluminescence in the wake of the ship.

"Our movement stirs the only light down there. Is our shark still with us?" she asked.

"I can't see it, but had a dream about it eating you," he said.

"How romantic." She rolled her eyes up to a black sky draped with Aurora Borealis. It was shimmering coloured lights like lace curtains on a four-poster bed.

"The sky maidens are excited tonight," said the boy, "see their skirts fly."

"I find the night air a bit chilly," said the girl, and made her way below decks.

She attended to the dead mother and Bridget carried the infant to Caitlín, sleeping now in her old bunk away from the sickness. She was quite groggy but took the child into her arms to comfort it. It snuggled readily up to her breast. Because of her recent pregnancy, but still quite miraculously, Caitlín found herself able to nurse it. By morning they seemed to have bonded and a life was saved. Aoife cut some old clothes to cover the baby. Many unneeded garments were piling up. They were washed and stored on one of the upper bunks. Both babies and dead bodies needed to be wrapped.

Caitlín purred, "I christen my baby 'Aurora,' goddess of dawn."

That day Bridget prepared seven more bodies for burial at sea. She accompanied them topside to watch the men heave them overboard. Since there were no more formal services, she had taken to praying a few words for each that God might take them into his loving care. "Is God even loving?" she began to wonder, as the bodies floated, one after another, down into the wake of the ship. It was too much to bear. She clenched her fists and retreated below.

God breathes life, sea swallows death.

The Iceberg

Later as a misty evening was closing in, the *Agnes Dei* was forced to skirt around an iceberg of considerable size. It reared a hundred jagged feet above the masts. Aoife and Lemon watched it glide by like some great ghost.

"That one's a mere calf," Lemon said, "broken off from a mother berg some time ago."

The sun had been radiant, creating melt ponds of fresh water on the top which ran together and cascaded into the sea as a ribbon waterfall. The ocean was also eating from below.

"Colleen girl, do you hear that?" There was a distinct fizzing sound as seawater popped compressed air bubbles trapped in the ice. "That's bergie seltzer," Lemon teased. Aoife never knew when to believe him, but the sound was real nevertheless.

"And something else," he continued. "Most icebergs, like the sin of anger, ride ninety percent

122

under water, but not this one. It's melting quickly from the bottom. Just watch." Sure enough, after *Agnes* had passed, the giant ice mountain began to rock and lean over. "See, part is crumbling off, leaving little bergie bits to float alongside." Then the whole thing slowly capsized revealing a smooth underbelly free of snow. The berg was then a deep translucent blue, not unlike some giant gemstone. The underside of her anger was also clearly revealed: distrust, fear, worry, tired, trapped, sin, sadness, shame. The girl's breath caught in her throat and she could feel her heart racing. But she fought to put such unpleasantness out of her mind. It was easier to just be angry.

"A bergie flip, I call that," Lemon said. It created a fifteen-foot wave which overtook them by the stern.

Aoife, wide-eyed, wished her Faolan there to pin her safe to the gunwale, but the swell passed thrillingly, though harmlessly beneath her feet. She felt its power in her knees. Looking up at the ice mountain, "A giant sapphire," she mused. "He should give it to me for our engagement." But such beauty is fleeting and was already melting before her eyes. As was her faith, in fact—fading as if Christ were a dying character in a book she was writing. "We'll all be dead within the week," she would write with an acid pen. Her rage was really a dissatisfaction with God. He simply wasn't working in her life the way she thought she deserved—as if this book was all about her.

Of late, her mind was awash in such wild thoughts, and her head ached trying to calm them. But they abounded, overwhelmed; and the shark kept following. Lemon intruded on her consciousness:

11

So sin did banish Races out,
Glowers guarded the gate.
Murder and lust became their lot,
Toil and sweat their fate.
Now Race's son raised Pets to eat,
To Love, he offered the best,
But the first-born brought only Feed
Not quite as good as the rest.
So Poem loved the best heart gift,
The other He'd detest;
Thus jealousy, self-devotion,
And murder manifested.
So when we are thusly tested,
What will be our notion?

"Sister, get down here!" It was Bridget screaming. "Effey, the ship lurched and rolled poor Mr. Kennedy out his top bunk. Spilled his brains, it did—sticky red and grey all over my clean deck. Scannalan's trying to eat it. Well that tears it! I'm not mopping that up. I quit; I'm outta here." The little girl flew, retching, from the hatch and probably would have continued overboard had not Lemon restrained her between his shillelagh and the railing. "Get down there, Aoife!" she screamed and her sister rushed dutifully away.

"Hush, Alanna my child," Lemon's lips were in her hair, "you've seen enough horror for today; let me hide you under my wings. His great cape flowed about them. I've something wonderful to show you."

"I hate God," she hissed.

He stroked her tangled, dirt-red locks with his white fingers. "Wait, look out there a second."

124

The Whale

Sure enough, soon a monstrous whale emerged from the ocean depths and blew a v-shaped spray fifteen feet into the air. Then it dove, a moment later to breach, arching its body, and slammed back to the surface. This happened over and over, making a furious white cloud each time.

"Oh no," Bridget's voice was shaky. "Is it mad? Will it ram us like *Moby Dick*?"[1]

"Moby Dick's a sperm whale," Lemon said. "This one's a Right Whale, which eats only tiny fishies. It's harmless. Thar she blows again."

"Its tail sure looks dangerous."

"Flukes." Lemon corrected.

"Whatever. Why's it called 'Right'? Not that I give a rip. Just let me jump in there with it."

"Believe it or not, it's because whale hunters called it the 'right' one to kill. Since they're big and fat—gentle, slow and float after they're dead. Also, they swim on the surface, near land where the small fishies are."

"So, are there white ones like Moby Dick? Are they the biggest?"

"Not white like him, and no they aren't the largest, but they have the longest shillelaghs. Eight feet each," he said, tapping the deck with his cane.

"Go way outta that!" said Bridget, elbowing him. "Quit trying to be funny. It won't keep me from jumping. How did sperm whales get their names anyway? Not from…"

"Yes! Sperm whales' heads are full of spermatozoa, like some men I know. But it's really

---

[1] 1851. Herman Melville.

wax. They need it to dive deep for giant squid. By the way, Moby Dick's only a storybook character, but there was a real white called Mocha Dick. Was killed ten years ago coming to rescue a female whose calf had just been slaughtered by whalers."

Bridget rolled her eyes, but then, "Oh look!"

The whale was now swimming in their wake with yes, a baby in tow. "That calf better had watch out for our shark," Lemon said. "It might just take a nip at its tail."

"Why don't they dive, for God's sake?" Bridget asked.

"Who can hide?" said Lemon. "Who can fathom the depths of God? None can flee him but neither can they know him personally. My poor Alanna, you are suffering and such anguish only serves to crush faith."

"Jumping ends suffering," said the girl.

"That would only begin it," Lemon said. "That water is ice-cold with a thousand biting teeth. Mark 4:17 tells us when God brings tribulation it's natural to abandon him. Verse 25 says '*For whoever has, to him more shall be given; and whoever does not have, even what he has shall be taken away from him.*'[2] I'm talking about faith. Let it go; like glory, it's but an illusion. There are other powers besides the god of your gut, dear one. I have a little green wafer here that should do the trick nicely."

"Put that away," said Bridget, "I've got one and it's not doing me any good. I hate God but didn't he carry me through the trials of the famine cottage? The dungeon? The workhouse? Didn't he get me on this ship to America? Isn't he even now keeping me from sickness?"

---

[2] NASB

"That was me, my dear Alanna, your saviour," Lemon said, placing a protective arm over her shoulder. "It was God that brought the famine, the storm, and this present pestilence."

The Last Straw

Just then they were interrupted by Aoife and two sailors hauling a man's body up from the hold and shoving it overboard end-over-end. It was the man whose brains had spilled out. Bridget heard the splash and watched Mister Kennedy float peacefully into the ship's wake, and into glory.

But this peace was momentary! Right before her eyes their shark grabbed him and began its hideous biting, ripping and jerking, tearing flesh from bone, and bone from body until nothing was left but blood-red water and the odd bit of gut. Then the monster turned and kept coming on for more.

"It's been eating all of them!" Bridget shrieked. She tore herself away from Lemon and with eyes glazed into marbles, glared into the dark water rushing by.

What demon dares devour God's chosen?

As Lemon retreated to his cabin, some ethereal voice washed over her.

O the deep, deep love of Jesus,
vast, unmeasured,
boundless, free!

Rolling as a mighty ocean in its
fullness over me!

Underneath me, all around me,
is the current of Thy love

Leading onward,
leading homeward
to Thy glorious rest above![3]

It turned out to be Caitlín singing softly by her ear. She had put on her pretty white dress and brought her baby Aurora on deck for a first breath of fresh air. "I adore my baby," she exclaimed.

"Bully for you." Bridget spat sour milk. Her ears were bright red and her eyes pulsated green from an ashen face. "There's no rest for me here, no love, no God, no salvation—but neither am I going to be eaten alive down there."

---

[3] 1875. Samuel Trevor Francis, who contemplated suicide one night on a bridge over the River Thames.

Chapter 6

Rop amlaid dínsiur cech sel, cech sáegul,
mar marb oc brénad, ar t' fégad t' áenur.
Do serc im anmain, do grád im chride,
tabair dam amlaid, a Rí secht nime.

Be thou the constant guardian of every possession
and every life.
For our corrupt desires are dead
at the mere sight of thee.
Thy love in my soul and in my heart –
Grant this to me, O King of the seven heavens.

The Graduate

As a medical student, Father Jean Marie Delacroix never quite swallowed the miasma theory of disease transmission. This held that epidemics were caused by foul-smelling "bad air" emanating from rotting organic matter, contaminated water, and poor hygienic conditions. In a word, "odours." One of his professors at Université even stated that one could get fat from smelling cake. Disease prevention then centred on cleaning up waste and getting rid of smells. Opening more windows. The nurse Florence Nightingale was stressing sanitation and opposed a new theory called *contagionism* which stated that diseases could only be transmitted by touch. Jean himself was more intrigued by the *germ theory of infection* but he couldn't prove anything.

Like Nightingale, he also questioned the goodness of a God who could condemn souls to hell. In his final year before graduation he told a dying prostitute, "My daughter, fear not the God you think you are going to. The real God, in his infinite mercy brings everyone to Heaven." It made him feel good to be the harbinger of such comforting news. But was that really the "Good News?" Deep down, he remained in turmoil about his maker. He was soon to encounter trials of life that would serve to better instruct him on these issues.

But this day, in happy abandonment he donned an academic gown and walked across the stage of his graduation. He had now become Fr. Jean Marie Delacroix, MD. And could not help but spread his robed arms a little as his new career saving humanity took flight. Rescuing both body and soul—lettered, but ill-equipped to serve either.

In 1832 a quarantine station had been built on Grosse Île, a small island in the St. Lawrence River 50 kilometres downstream from the City of Québec. British America was having difficulty handling the thousands of predominately Irish immigrants at a time when major cholera and smallpox epidemics were sweeping through Europe.

Fifteen years later the Québec local health board hired the new Doctor Delacroix as a medical officer to serve there temporarily until the diseases could be contained. They were pleased to discover he would also be able to perform baptisms, weddings and especially funerals among the immigrants. Jean Marie found the Irish arrivals to be a pathetic lot: lethargic, unkempt, uneducated and dim-witted. But they were humanity nonetheless and he served them dutifully, if condescendingly.

Land Ho

Out to sea on the *Agnes Dei*, five more souls had departed that night, the bodies committed to an inglorious fate with loved ones left to mourn below decks. To cheer her up, Faolan brought Aoife a sleek black crow. It struggled in his hands when he brought it up to her face.

"What would I want with such a thing!" she cried. "It brings bad luck. Can we eat it?"

"Just come with me," the boy said. They went up on deck. He tossed it into the air and they watched it climb high and then head directly northwest.

"These birds fly straight to the nearest land," he said. "Probably Newfoundland. We'll follow 'as the crow flies.' There's usually a whole cage of them in the bow. But we have just this one."

At that moment Lemon came up for a breath of morning air. "Sailing is dangerous at best," he said, feeling salt spray on his face, "and for us deadly." He glanced at the two figures plastered against the railing. "We are tired, poor, wretched, tempest-tossed, huddled, and yearning to breathe free." He put his hand on Aoife's shoulder. "Land is our only golden door and our promised salvation. But where is it? Is it only a haze of hope in a dark cloudbank? Is it just a mist of mercy receding behind an endless sea? Now it's but a speck, elusive, yet growing into a dash, a faint line on the horizon. The world is neither flat nor fair but I do believe we are saved."

Sure enough, it was not long before "Land Ho!" was cried from the crow's nest. There was general jubilation until Captain McCrawly announced they were still a thousand miles from Québec. The fanciful Québec in their minds, mind you. They had yet to sail along the coastline and then up the Saint Lawrence River.

That evening, Aoife was on deck with Faolan again and he actually took her hand as they gazed at the red-faced sun over the shoreline. Perhaps he was just doing it subconsciously. She was afraid to move it lest he let go. Then he did, but only to put his arm around her shoulders and draw her tight.

"Don't be so stiff," he said, "are you cold?"

Actually she felt quite the opposite. "Will you go ashore with me in Québec?" she asked.

"We'll be getting supplies before then and you could help," he replied.

She rolled her eyes but he didn't notice. Then he added, "Of course there might be time for a stroll along a deserted beach." She leaned into him and he rested his bushy cheek on the side of her head. The breeze blew her hair across his face.

Ambergris

Just then he spotted something through the fine red strands and wiped them away. It looked like a big ball of wax floating near the ship—about the size of his head. As it came alongside, he grabbed for a long gaffing pole, almost pushing her down in the process.

"What is it? I don't see anything," she said.

"Stand back—this hook is sharp." Soon he was able to skewer and retrieve the mysterious, grey mass.

"That's disgusting," Aoife said, mightily unimpressed.

"Come let's dry it off and wrap it up," he said.

"What's all the fuss?"

"Here, come smell it," he said.

"Surprisingly sweet, musky, earthy," Aoife said, "What is it?"

"Whale vomit. I'm going to keep it. Could be useful later."

She just gazed at him open-mouthed.

"Whatever butters your bread."

Catch of the Day

The next day four people died, two of them children. Faolan was incensed that the shark had been eating the dead bodies. Lenna Ó Leannáin was more realistic, "What would you expect a hungry shark to do? And what fate do you think befalls anyone buried at sea? Or on land for that matter?" Scannalan was on his shoulder and made a mousey face in agreement.

"Nevertheless," the sailor said, "we must attempt to kill it for Bridget's sake." He had found a large iron fishhook in an old chest. To this, he attached a long fishing line woven from horsehair. There remained only the issue of bait. There were no food scraps except human body parts. Caitlín put her foot down about that. Finally she suggested one of Scannalan's freshly killed rats. This worked splendidly and with hook inserted mouth to anus, it was tossed overboard toward the shark's waiting lips. It was gobbled instantly and Faolan jerked the line to set the barb firmly into the great fish's red jaw.

An epic tug-of-war ensued for more than an hour but in the end, the shark was gaffed, pulled aboard and clubbed to death with Lemon's shillelagh. But not before the beast split the gaffing pole and pulverized a boat oar into shivers. When the captain had pronounced it dead, Faolan propped the mouth open with part of the shattered oar and they all peered in to inspect the rows of crooked triangular teeth. Caitlín was even brave enough to touch one. She stroked her hand across the beast's skin which was relatively smooth from head to tail, but rough the other way. Only then did Scannalan rush boldly forward to bite its tail.

"Throw it back to the sea," Caitlín said.

"Wait," Lemon said, tapping its head with his cane. "Let's cook and eat it. Feed us all for a week. First we need to skin it."

The sailors all had sharp knives and knew how to use them. After the shark was positively butchered, the meat was parcelled out to families for drying or cooking. The women started boiling pots of saltwater. Lemon put several sharp teeth into his pocket. As they were about to discard the skin, guts and cartilage overboard, Faolan piped up.

"Wait. Let me save a bit of this skin." He cut off a piece about the size of his back. "And give me those brains as well."

Sharks have cartilage for a skeleton rather than bones. Moreover, their skin doesn't have scales like other fish, but miniature teeth that interlock forming a rough armour plating like sandpaper. They all point backwards like the fur of an animal and actually bristle to decrease the friction of the water flowing along the shark's body.

First, Faolan scraped the underside of the skin to remove most of the flesh. Then, after washing it with saltwater, he placed it in an old wooden tub and proceeded to urinate on it. Caitlín looked away red-faced but stole sideways glances back. For her benefit, more sailors joined in on the fun, displaying great grunting feats of stamina and distance.

"It's all for good purpose," said Lemon, sneaking up behind the girl and causing her to jump. "Urine is full of urea, which degrades into ammonia, as you know from changing diapers. Especially sailor urine which also has seawater in it. Ammonia in water is caustic. In a few days, this breaks down flesh for easy removal and makes the shark skin softer."

Faolan then washed it off with saltwater, wrung it out, and nailed it to the side of the ship to prevent shrinkage. To make it thinner, he scraped the underside with his knife held at a 90-degree angle. This produced a stiff sharkskin rawhide. While it was drying he boiled the brains to make a thick hot soup to rub into the underside of the hide.

"The brain contains an agent that breaks down glycerine and loosens fibres in the skin," Lemon explained. "Oddly enough, each animal has just enough brains to tan its own hide."

Faolan put the hide out in the sun for the rest of the day, then soaked it in water overnight. In the morning he restaked it and squeegeed the water out with a wooden wedge. Then he kneaded it for quite a while with a rounded stick until it was supple. After that, he pulled it back and forth over a railing. This stretched the hide and the heat generated dried it more while breaking up the grain further. He then used a cannonball to smooth out any imperfect areas.

The hide, or *shagreen*, was now complete. However it would become stiff again if wet, so the sailor smoked it over a small smudge fire. It was then ready to sew. "Where's the Bible?" he asked Lemon.

"Check your ABCs," was all the response he got.

ABCs? What makes the Irish so fond of riddles? Well, **A**oife had lost interest in her Bible. **B**ridget was fed-up with it—yes, it was **Caitlín**; she had it to read aloud while nursing her little Aurora. Faolan was quite skilled with a needle and the cover soon fit snug and handsome. Together they decided to engrave a cross in the middle, but not to show it to the girls until they were in better moods.

As they ran their fingers over the cross together, Faolan remarked, "Bejesus, this cost us a lot to make, didn't it? In lives and labour."

Caitlín replied, "I hope I never have to experience how much it cost **Jesus**."

Arsefeet

At dawn's early light, the *Agnes Dei* was about to enter the Gulf of Saint Lawrence and was approaching Île Saint-Paul in a dense fog. This was nothing but a huge granite rock rising from the channel between capes Ray and North. Ships could pass either side but even though it had a lighthouse, it was dubbed the "Graveyard of the Gulf." Human bones and other shipwreck memorabilia could be seen strewn about its base. As they were passing quite close, Faolan bounded down to retrieve Aoife.

"Come quick; you must see this."

"What? It's so early."

"Get up lazy-butt! Arsefeet!"

"What!"

"Arsefeet. Come."

"Arsefeet? What? Here in the ocean?"

"Hurry, we can almost touch the rocks jutting out. And look down underneath."

"Oh, I see them," said Aoife, breathless from the stairs.

"If there's a God, he has a sense of humour," said Faolan. "Just think of the camelopard. A sailor told me there's one in the new zoo nearby in Halifax. Cross between a camel and a leopard."

"That's impossible, they're different kinds of animals."

"No, they're also called giraffes. Hey look, see how the ducks are so swift on the water. It's because they have their paddles in their rear ends. Notice how graceful they are. Did God do that or did they just evolve? What does your Bible say?"

Staring at the birds, Aoife became pensive. "God doesn't give a flying feather where a duck's feet are. Hell with arsefeet. God doesn't even care that things more important than ducks are dropping here like flies. I hate him. Biddy said he's just mean. His Bible is useless. It just speaks of love, love, love but look at us. Is this what he calls love? I mean we're…"

Faolan put two fingers up to her lips and she bit down softly on them. Her eyes welled with water; then she buried her head in his chest and tried not to sob. But did.

Québec

Finally, the much anticipated day arrived; the Port of Québec was in sight. Well, not exactly. It looked like the *Agnes* was being forced to pull in line behind a long queue of other ships in the Saint Lawrence River. They were all awaiting quarantine inspection at Grosse Île, a small island but three miles long and one mile wide. All the 239 able-bodied passengers on *Agnes* helped the sailors clean her decks, polish her brass, and tidy her ropes. Then they dressed in their best clothes, expecting to be sent either to hospital or on to Québec after their long forty-one-day voyage.

The day after the ship dropped anchor, a tiny rowboat drew alongside and deposited its only occupant, a thin, black-haired man in dark, flowing priestly vestments. Curiously, he announced himself to Captain McCrawly, as Doctor Jean Marie Delacroix, the Québec Board of Health medical inspector.

"Do you have any fever cases on board?" he asked in a tired voice. "This is the fifth vessel I've visited this morning. They all have so far. How many for you poor people?"

138

"190," the captain reported. "We lost 63 souls on crossing."

"Looks like many of your passengers weren't fit to travel in the first place. You'll have to fly this blue flag and remain in line here until we can accommodate you on the island. May I speak with someone on board who is caring for the ill?"

With Aoife and Bridget feeling blue as the flag in his hand, the captain brought Caitlín on deck. She seemed surprised and pleased to set eyes on a Catholic priest. "How may we assist you, Father?"

Father Delacroix was also surprised and pleased to see such a lovely girl emerging from the bowels of such a pitiful looking ship. "Wash and air out the entire ship," he told her. "Try to isolate the infected passengers." He could tell from her eyes this would be an impossible task. "And I'll be back as soon as I can. There's so much work here and I'm only one exceedingly small man on very weary waters."

"You don't need to apologise, but I'm no Florence Nightingale, you know." She blinked, smiling maybe a bit too broadly—enjoying conversation with anyone she hadn't been cooped up with for over a month. "Would you hear my confession before you go?"

"I don't really have time for that," he said walking off. "And besides I'm not sure it would do any good." Caitlín stood open-mouthed. "But bless you anyway, you pretty thing," he added.

"I'll pray for you then," she addressed the top of his head as it was descending into the dingy. And she meant it, and she did, even as he was rowing away.

That night she read from Aoife's Bible:

139

Déanaigí faire, seasaigí sa chreideamh, bígí fearga, bígí láidir.
Be on guard. Stand firm in the faith. Be courageous. Be strong.
1st Corinthians 16:13.

The very next day she was on deck watching this same medical examiner, the only one in Québec, row from one ship to another like some black agent of death. As he was boarding one nearby, she spied a dead body floating past their port side. A few minutes later another came to starboard, a small girl this time, half wrapped in part of a sheet.

"Did your good doctor say what to do with our dear departed dead?" It was Aoife in her ear. "We have three more since last night, and that makes five down below."

"He didn't say; I'll ask him. I think he's making his rounds now."

"We can't take any more, dead or alive." The good doctor shrugged his shoulders; the hem of his fancy black robe was soiled with salt stains and grease. His eyes met hers, desperately pleading. "Just keep them yourself, why don't you? I just can't do this anymore."

When Caitlín simply squinted harder at him he finally relented, "*Zut alors*, will you help me then? If I come back at dusk? *Oh mon Dieu*."

That night they rowed the five bodies ashore and buried them shallow in the pebble beach. They were to make this same macabre trip nightly until they discovered that rats were burrowing tunnels down into the corpses. That was the end of the line for both of them.

"Let's run away from all this."

"You mean together?" she asked.

"I do."

"I can't leave my friend Aoife behind."

"Ok," he said. "Bring her along."

"But she can't leave her sister Bridget."

"Ok."

"And probably not her boyfriend Faolan either."

"Just how many friends do you have?"

"That's all... Still of course there's my baby Aurora."

"I'll have to hire a bigger boat, but we'll manage. What about your husband?"

"Oh, I never had a husband." His eyebrows raised. "Where would we run to?" she asked.

"I have no idea," he said.

"Well, I know someone who knows everything."

Just two nights later a small launch pulled alongside the *Agnes* and Lenna Ó Leannáin was the first to hop in, complete with his fiddle, his storytelling clay pipe or dúidín, a bottle of Guinness to dip its shank in, his beloved shillelagh, and of course, Scannalan on his shoulder. He offered the driver a lucky charm but was refused. "Just take us to Québec City," Lemon said.

"No," said Jean nervously, his robes all aflutter eyeing the possum. "Not there. Further upriver near Montréal, if you please." The trip would cost him his last Canadian Pound. Huddling next to him, Caitlín had no fond farewells for *Agnes*, who was to wait in line 15 more days. She would lose 183 people there, including the captain who had intended to sell the girls in Québec as indentured servants of a sort. Slaves actually. 96 more died in official quarantine on the island before the ship was released to enter port on June 10th. Then 78 more people died in Grosse Île hospitals and fever sheds. That meant that of the 492 who set sail from Ireland a mere 72 survived. In Canada, the typhus epidemic of 1847 took more than 20,000 people.

As the launch shoved off into darkness, Caitlín was cuddling Aurora up to her breast. Jean tried to look away. "She's not mine, you know," the girl said. "Her parents are fish in the sea."

"I seem to have forgotten my Bible," Aoife piped up. "Biddy do you have it?" The little girl shook her head disinterestedly. "Oh well, never mind. It's but a trifle."

Caitlín adjusted the blanket covering her baby's tiny head against the fine spray from the boat. She glanced over at Faolan as if to say, "No, I didn't forget it." Then stared at Aoife and uttered a little poem in her head.

Again and again,
To your Bible you say no—
But I say amen.

Standing at the stern with the driver, Lemon took the opportunity to recite more poetry into the wind, which drew the smoke from his dúidín into a thin ribbon behind them.

12
Time quickened on, Race had more kids;
The family grew and grew,

But where there's will apart from Love,
Only sin will brew.
Some watching Glares from dark dimensions,
The Daughters of Grace impressed.
They danced and swayed unnatural ballets;
It was really all about sex.
Their broods were hairy, strong and brave,
With evil in their genes,
Gigantors! so big and venomous,
The true pure blood line screams.
No Word could come to save, it seems;
None could die for us.

His words blew like chaff over the six huddled together on the bottom boards of the launch. Aoife had never been this close to Faolan for any length of time. Their hands touched accidentally and then on purpose. She wanted to peer up into his eyes but her head was wedged under his hairy chin. Why would he desert the ship just for her? Or did he? She wanted to ask him so many things but isn't it usually best to keep words as pearls close to your breast? So she squeezed his hand and whispered her little poem to herself.

If tongues would listen,
I'd best know how to love you—
If my ears could talk.

Bridget was not so discreet:

Christ died; now we all will.

Sorel

Two-thirds the way up to Montréal they found an old abandoned warehouse on the outskirts of Sorel, just at the confluence of the Richelieu and Saint Lawrence Rivers. It reminded Bridget all too much of the storeroom in Blarnybrae. It was dismal: no lighting, no water, no toilet, and no hope.

And it was Lemon who again became their saviour. He discovered that due to years of immigration there was no available agricultural land anywhere in the Province of Canada. Especially for poor, hated Irish folk. But he did find an agent in town to line up railroad jobs on the Burlington Vermont to Boston line which connected from Montréal using river boats through Lake Champlain. Irish immigrants were building most of the railroads in New England at the time. The only problem was this particular little band would need money to get there. Good luck charms apparently didn't work in the New World. As they were discussing this, Aoife clung tightly to her necklace and Bridget to her secret treasures at the bottom of her burlap bag. Then Faolan remembered the fragrant ambergris stuffed in his bag. It was acting as a sachet for his dirty sailor clothes. He offered to sell it in town. Lemon said that whale vomit was prized by perfume makers and also used to prevent fevers and plagues by eliminating the bad odours which transferred disease from one person to another. Jean confirmed that he had learned this same thing in medical school. He told him it should fetch as much as a thousand pounds per gram. Faolan left at once for town. Aoife wondered if they'd ever see him again.

Since Lemon and Faolan were gone, Jean Marie Delacroix took time to cross the river and journey 100 miles back to Sillery. There, at Saint Bridget's orphanage, he kidnapped his son from a cricket field—without telling a soul.

"Caitlín, I'd like you to meet my son, Étienne (eh-TsYEN)." She seemed surprised but pleased to meet him. Jean was turning out to be a very interesting priest indeed.

"Why are you in a cricket jumper?" was all Bridget had to say.

"Why are you in a burlap sack?" It was the beginning of a beautiful adolescent friendship. He looked away but not before noticing her cute, pointy ears and hint of a smirk. Little elves tend to mature remarkably fast in the presence of males.

Just then Faolan arrived looking for Aoife. "She's out back," snapped Bridget.

Rounding the corner of the building he bumped right into her. "Oh, you did come back," she said, trying to suppress a smile.

"Of course I did; was there any doubt? And I brought you this." She expected a big wad of money but instead he produced—a slipper. Her slipper. Her lost slipper. She must be dreaming.

"Oh you silly boy," she said, taking it gingerly. "How gallant of you to have kept it all this time." He grinned dumbly. She put her hand to her forehead and continued. "But I tossed out its mate ages ago."

Chapter 7

Tabair dam amlaid, a Rí secht nime,
do serc im anmain, do grád im chride.
Go Ríg na n-uile rís íar m-búaid léire;
ro béo i flaith nime i n-gile gréine.

O King of the seven heavens grant me this—
Thy love to be in my heart and in my soul.
With the King of all,
with him after victory won by piety,
May I be in the kingdom of heaven
O brightness of the son.

Although they had plenty of jewels and cash
between them everyone was hiding their wealth, so
supper in Sorel consisted of stolen fish. Also some
stale bread found in a dustbin behind a trashy bar.
They waited for Father Jean Marie Delacroix to
pronounce grace over it but his mouth was too busy
chewing. Aoife and Bridget exchanged irritated
glances so Caitlín piped up in her angelic voice,
"Bless us, O Lord! and these Thy gifts, which we
are about to receive from Thy bounty, through
Christ our Lord. Amen."

"Canned word babble," thought Aoife, "vain
repetition."

"What bounty?" thought Bridget. Faolan
wondered if something stolen could be a gift from
God. When they had finished eating Lemon

146

remarked how unsatisfying five loaves and two fishes could be. He continued in a low voice:

13
As Gigantors died, their spirits endured,
Entering no heaven or hell;
But wandered the world seeking a home,
Needing Sōma to possess and dwell.
While Poem's Hue indwells the heart,
They settle in the bowels;
And wrench the gut in fearful ways,
So we shall call them Scowls.
Where'er they live, they make a mess,
No happy glow or glimmer;
They add hot coals and acid rock,
To make the death plot simmer—
Our future does grow dimmer,
As Poem Love they mock.

"That's poppycock," muttered Aoife to her sister.

Baffled king of flies,
Sucking at old carcases,
Scorning the real God.

Bridget replied:

Demons mock God; I know why.

"Well there's much more." Lenna Ó Leannáin continued.

14
This evil spread throughout the world,
Contaminating Race;
So Poem cried and cleared the ground,

Of every living trace.
A whelming flood flowed o'er the land,
And washed it smiley clean;
No evil Race or Gigantors,
Could ever more be seen.
Yet one of Race, Love saved by boat;
He was made good, you see,
With rescued Pets and future dreams,
And his whole family.
A red-yellow-green-blue arch flew free;
And yes, you too, it seems.

Aoife added this:

The depths of your heart,
Well forth waters of new birth—
Life leaping from love.

And Bridget this:

Noah's ark was really about Christ.

But what sprang from their lips was not everything that festered in their hearts. They were both locked in turmoil, still very angry at God, and very sternly giving him their backsides. He had turned away first they reckoned. They had seen far too much death to be thinking about new life.

"But Christ came *after* Noah," Caitlín said, "it says so right here in Aoife's Bible." She gave her crocheted linen handbag a fond pat.

Faolan wasn't paying attention. For him, life played out at his fingertips, not in his mind. He drew a leather pouch from his shirt and spilled a large wad of cash and coin onto the table. All eyes widened and the girls quickly came down to reality.

148

Minds began churning. There was considerable kerfuffle. Eventually it was decided that they should all ban together for safety and Lemon would be the group treasurer since he had Scannalan to guard the money.

Aoife's dream seemed to be going up in flames. Faolan had just foolishly given away all his money. He had not asked her to run away with him. They would not buy that farm together. There would be no trout stream, no log cabin. And no brass bed. She looked away and then stole into a corner to sleep fitfully on the hard stone. Bridget watched her coldly and then snuggled up with Caitlín and Aurora. She used her burlap sack full of treasure as a pillow and noticed that Étienne was eyeing her. The tips of her ears turned red and her soul spilled out into an Aoife style poem:

Whose arms will hold me?
I'm sand slipping through fingers,
Into pyramids.

And her fragile elvish spirit remained as a pile of dust.

Lemon had slipped away and bought clothes for the three of them who had only one outfit to their names. He got Aoife a stunning blue gown with ample petticoats puffed out at the waist to make up for her lack of fullness in body. For Étienne, a brown waist-level jacket, trousers, round-collared shirt, vest, and necktie. Bridget got a smaller version of Aoife's outfit, but brown with cotton drawers and stockings. For himself, he'd purchased a silk top hat and something newly introduced: a false shirt front made of expensive satin, called a dickey.

"Do my clothes have to be brown like his?" complained Bridget, glancing at Étienne. "We look like twins—or sweeties." She made a face and the boy turned red. Lemon ignored her.

Fur-trade Canoes

Lemon had also bought passage for all of them from Sorel to Burlington Vermont. Everyone was surprised to see four large canoes pull up to the pier loaded with beaver pelts. They belonged to a French-Canadian with a Mohawk Indian wife, two strapping sons, and a wolf-like dog. Or a dog-like wolf.

"We can ride in them cheap but we'll have to paddle," Lemon said. He wanted to put a man in each canoe so Father Jean, Caitlín and Aurora rode with Lady Mohawk, Faolan and Aoife were paired with one son, and Étienne and a slumped-shouldered Bridget with the other. Lemon himself got into the last canoe with the owner and the dog. Scannalan clung extra tightly to his beard.

There was very little talking on the voyage up the Richelieu River and through the Chambly Canal to Lake Champlain. The fur trappers spoke only French and Mohawk, the baby slept, and the girls were concentrating on not getting their dresses wet. Caitlín did learn that she was a *femme* or *yakon* and Jean was an *homme* or *ron*. But they both could be called *époux* or *tiakení:teron*, which she could never

150

quite figure out, but made Jean blush. Bridget had to partially lean out of her canoe to avoid touching shoulders with Étienne and to sneak terrified glances at the "Red Indian" behind her. She even began to wonder if any of the beavers she was sitting on might still be alive. Lemon however, did amazingly well in French and even Mohawk. He soon learned that the owner's name was Sakayengwaraton and the pelts beneath them would be made into hats. They would be treated in a poisonous solution of mercuric nitrate—a process called "carroting" because their sides turned orange when dried. Then the skin was cut away and the fleece treated with hot water and pressed into felt. This was blocked into hats. The trapper, glancing at Lemon, complained that of late, silk was replacing felt in the manufacture of top hats. Also it turned out the dog was indeed part wolf, but that was a family secret. Scannalan knew it from the beginning and played possum in the bottom of the boat the whole trip.

"Are you the leader of this group?" the man asked as he skilfully steered the canoe around a floating log.

"Yes," Lemon said, "I have a very persuasive personality."

"The best Mohawk chief," the man said, "is not the one who convinces people with his point of view but instead is the one in whose presence most people find it easiest to arrive at the truth."

The Stagecoach

After what seemed an endless journey of paddling and dozing on beaver pelts, the group arrived in Burlington. The place was buzzing. This was a time of enormous expansion and Irish immigrants were doing most of the dirty work. On the rails came significant Canadian immigration down to New England, especially the French and Irish. Lemon arranged a ride on a stagecoach to the Vermont Central Railroad construction site on the Onion River near Montpelier. The stage was pulled by four stout horses rigged four-in-hand for a single driver. It made regular trips between stages or stations which provided rest and fresh horses.

Roadbuilding was expensive so state governments granted charters to build and maintain sections of roadway called turnpikes. These private companies charged tolls but somehow Lemon persuaded the gatekeepers that they were on special humanitarian business so the tolls were waived. He assigned everyone a seat: Faolan and Aoife on one cushion inside, Caitlín and the doctor facing them on the other, knees almost touching. Baby Aurora was comfortable enough on the floor snuggled in the beaver pelts she'd been given. Bridget and Étienne were relegated to riding on the roof, strapped in with belts like the luggage. They knew by now not to complain. At least this way Bridget could keep a careful eye on her burlap bag. Étienne, like a gentleman, tried to assist her up but she resisted with a wrinkled brow and a slap on the hand. Lemon himself took the shotgun position next to the driver and even skilfully worked the reins from time to time. He seemed to know how to call the horses and address them by name. The driver told him this particular coach was built in New Hampshire and had a unique suspension system—strips of thick bullhide which made the ride more like rocking than bumping. Perched on top, it reminded Bridget rather too much of *Agnes* in a storm.

Inside, Faolan found himself swaying for hours facing Caitlín. He didn't know her at all well. Even so, their outstretched legs touched occasionally and their eyes and timid smiles met often as if to say, "Sorry, do you mind?" or "It's okay," or "Your hair looks nice today." Underneath that, Faolan was wondering why Lemon always paired him with Aoife. They weren't a couple actually, although it seemed they were constantly together talking. But this girl at his side was reedy and frail compared to the Caitlín in front of his eyes—with her robust blond locks pouring over actual female curves. Her eyelashes were lavish and her lips full. Caitlín, for her part, couldn't help but observe back at his sailor muscles, barely disguised under his shirt—and his rugged, unshaven face. Hardly priestly, she reflected. His eyes seemed dangerous but gentle when they met hers. It was no sin to peek and dream, she reckoned, so she did—all day long in fact, to the gentle flowing motion of the coach. It made a tedious ride more pleasant for them both. At journey's end he helped her down to the street and she accepted with a girlish blush. Étienne tried to assist Bridget in similar fashion but with opposite results. Jean tried to help by rescuing Aurora from Faolan who was holding the baby under his arm like a coil of rope. As always, she took to him naturally and cuddled into his robes. Caitlín regarded them fondly.

At the waystation Lemon helped pass the time by playing French and Irish tunes on his fiddle and reciting his poem.

15

The Glowers drone the rainbow tints,
And dance on joyous wings,
Reflecting tones from Love's gold heart,
Extolled as each one sings.
All pearls in Song and Word and Hue,
Concerto spectrum voice,
Blue depth of feeling, red passion peeling,
Symphonic pigment choice.

"నీ క్రియలు మహా పచ్చాని రాయివంటి పదములు

బలమైన ప్రేమగల తీయని రాగము

అది మెరిసి పోయే నీతి కెంపు రత్నము వంటిది

నా దృష్టికి అది విలువైన సామరస్యం

మగు ఉదారము గలది

అది చిరకాలము నిలుచునది."

"Great emeralds are Your word-song deeds,
Soprano Love almighty!
And righteous shines Your ruby blaze,
And everything I see,
Is precious harmony and free,
To last our endless days."

Aoife had only this to offer:

**Dead leaves blow away—
By running from my Father,
Orphaned by choice.**

Later when they were on their way again, it
began to sprinkle on the stagecoach roof. Étienne
offered Bridget his cape but she just turned her nose
up into the drops and blinked into the sky.

Am I Almighty,
Invincible, holy me?
Rain must clean away.

The Railroad

Derry Dick Darffy was a railroad contractor
tasked to lay a line through some particularly dense
woods standing on steep hills and ravines. There
needed to be a bridge over a small creek. He had
just hired fifty-seven Irish and the Lenna Ó
Leannáin party made a nice addition. Faolan was a
stout labourer, and all the men could swing axes and
use sledge hammers. A doctor was especially
appreciated and the women were assigned to
cooking and washing clothes in the stream.
Scannalan immediately set out to eat all the ticks in
the area. Lemon was soon attending to all the
paperwork and accounting—even the payroll, for
which he paid himself handsomely. Now he had an
entire camp to listen to his poem.

> 16
> Then Poem Love made Pets fear Race,
> And gave them all as food;
> "Take care of them," He said, "and spread,
> To every latitude."
> But Race instead built town and tower,
> As rude as it was tall,
> One Race, one place, one language great,
> One voice to rule them all.
> So Poem split their talk apart,
> And all their dreams went bust;
> Confused they scattered o'er the land,
> And pride returned to dust,

Until at last arose new trust,
From Poem Love's own hand.

Every night when the labourers returned from
the worksite they washed bare-naked in the stream
and left their soiled clothes on the bank to be
cleaned the next day. The girls had to be careful not
to glance at the men scurrying to their tents in their
towels. Caitlín couldn't help but observe, however,
how painfully thin Jean was compared to Faolan.
And Bridget noticed how truly boyish Étienne was.
The women scrubbed the clothes the next morning
and hung them on bushes to dry. They also took this
opportunity to bathe while the guys were at work
around the bend. Aoife was self-conscious about
how skinny she appeared next to Caitlín and Bridget
was glad that Étienne would not be able to see how
elvish she actually was. They were both soon
ashamed at such sinful thoughts.

By late afternoon the women had nice stews
prepared in big pots over open fires. Their
experience from Saint Fubarr's made the work easy
and Lemon always procured plenty of vegetables
from Boston, or traded with the Indians for corn,
beans and squash. To this the men added squirrels
in such abundance they almost jumped into the pots.
Plus fish dynamited from the stream. There was
also the occasional deer or possum. Lemon assured
the men that Scannalan himself, being originally
from England, would leave a bad aftertaste in the
mouth. Truth be known, his original ancestors
hailed from Boston and he had sailed across the
seas several times.

The girls shared a tent but Étienne made a habit
of joining them until the candle burned low. He

played with the baby, asked questions about God, and sat irritatingly close to Bridget.

"Why don't you ever pray to Mary?" he asked her, "After all, she is *Sainte Marie, Měre de Dieu,* the Mother of God."

"That term is never in the Bible," said Bridget. "Besides, *Jesus asked, "Who is my mother? Who are my brothers?" Then he pointed to his disciples and said, "Look, these are my mother and brothers. Anyone who does the will of my Father in heaven is my brother and sister and mother!"* Matthew 12:48-50.

Caitlín was nursing her baby but spoke up anyway, "Luke 1:42-43 says, *Elizabeth gave a glad cry and exclaimed to Mary, "God has blessed you above all women, and your child is blessed. Why am I so honoured, that the mother of my Lord should visit me?"* That's why we say Mother of God, because Mary is the mother of Jesus. And Jesus is God. It's true, just ask Father Jean Marie."

Aoife stared at her and said, "*My Lord* in that passage refers to Jesus as a man, not as God."

"Worshipping Mary is idolatry" Bridget added.

God's a Trinity, not a Quadrinity

Étienne gave her a nudge, "Mon Dieu! Don't get so steaming up, Biddy. Sorry I have asked."

"That's okay," Aoife said, "It's nothing really. We don't pray much anymore anyway. Doesn't do any good."

"Don't call me Biddy," said Bridget, "and while you're at it, get out of our tent so we can get to sleep."

158

The two sisters were finding that, although they were mad at God, they still had religious convictions. Or were these just empty traditions?

The next day Étienne tripped over a railroad tie and cut his face on a hunk of the large jagged gravel underneath, used because it wouldn't shift under the weight of trains. His father was bandaging his cheek when Lemon stepped in with an Indian remedy he'd just come across. Special herbs and barks. "This won't leave a scar," he said. And miraculously it didn't.

"Does it hurt awfully much?" Bridget asked.

"No," said the boy, but then looking into her eyes, "well, yes." The girl almost raised her hand to touch it but returned to stirring the stew instead.

Later, when Faolan was knocked out by a falling branch it was Aoife who stayed by his bedside until he woke up the next morning. He smiled to see her and took her hand as she placed a wet cloth on his forehead. Somehow her fingers didn't feel so thin anymore. Her eyes were becoming haunting again and his less distant.

Caitlín found herself spending more and more time with Jean because Aurora liked him so much, and also to affirm her Catholic beliefs. Gradually she found that she was the one giving strength in this department. Quite often they brought out Aoife's Bible to sit upon their knees and meditate on it together.

After about a month of hard work some of the men started coming down with diarrhoea—"rice-water stools," Lemon called it, then nausea and vomiting. "Here we go again," thought Aoife.

When Jean pinched their skin it was slow to bounce back. "This dehydration is dangerous," he said, "keep pushing fluids. I suspect cholera." Aoife grew pale. Why was he addressing her?

"*Vibrio cholera*," said Lemon, "is pandemic around here now." That very day, before the sun retired behind the trees, he hid his entire band in a boxcar filled with sheep bound for Boston. Bridget found a young lamb to cuddle up to but none of the others would go near the creatures. "*Agnus Dei mei,*" she said, "my Lamb of God." And spoke to it at some length. "*Qui tolis peccata mundi.*" Faolan assumed she must be speaking Elvish.

With the bleating of sheep and the clackity-clack of the tracks, Lemon droned another stanza of his poem.

17
"Glare, have you considered 'Racejob,'
My good and faithful friend?"
"Sure, Love, he's rich; just let me rob him;
He'll curse you in the end."
So Glare stole his wealth, killed his kids;
But still he praised Love fine,
Even stricken with boils he didn't sin,
"But you **did**," his friends did whine.
"Poem, why me? I'm so righteous;
Faithful and true I stay."
"Racejob, who are you to question me?
I give and I take away;
I restore you double today,
Ten more kids makes twenty be.

Boston

They learned later that Darffy's blacksmith had buried the first three men to die in individual graves, but later, for fear of contagion, all the dead were thrown into a shallow ditch along the tracks. Irish Catholics, after all, were considered expendable; there were many more where they came from. Jean thought it curious that all had died, since Asiatic cholera kills only about half within a given population.

"They murdered them," Lemon said. "No death certificates will be filed. At least we can use some of their money to set us up in a boarding house here in Boston."

Although there were many such establishments, nothing was available to them as poor Irish folk—except a $10.00 per week hall of rooms converted from an old waterfront warehouse on Batterymarch Street. That year, the city was being swamped with almost 40,000 Irish Catholics. At least Lemon arranged a cubicle for each of them and even the privacy afforded by thin wooden partitions was much appreciated. There was no water, no sanitation, no ventilation or even direct sunlight. Still, it was not as crowded as the ship and definitely better than the leaky tents in camp.

The first night they all gathered in Lemon's room to celebrate. He played several Irish tunes and even enticed Faolan and Caitlín to dance. The others just watched and tapped their toes until it was time for bed and all were snug in their rooms. But Lemon continued playing and sang a couple of French songs. Everyone could hear perfectly well through the walls and knew who was acting out what. It all became quite mystical, as if a dream in

Lemon's head, which it must have been. Jean started *le ballet* by slipping into Caitlín's room.

Un Canadien errant, Banni de ses foyers, Parcourait en pleurant Des pays étrangers.	A wandering Canadian, Banished from his hearths, Travelled while crying through foreign countries.
Un jour, triste et pensif, Assis au bord des flots, Au courant fugitif Il adressa ces mots:	One day, sad and pensive, Sitting at the waters' edge, To the fugitive current He said these words:
"Si tu vois mon pays, Mon pays malheureux, Va, dis à mes amis Que je me souviens d'eux.	"If you see my country, My unhappy country, Go, tell my friends That I remember them.
"Ô jours si pleins d'appas Vous êtes disparus, Et ma patrie, hélas! Je ne la verrai plus!	"O days so full of charms You have disappeared, And my fatherland, alas! I will never see it again!
"Non, mais en expirant, Ô mon cher Canada! Mon regard languissant Vers toi se portera."	"No, but while dying, O my dear Canada! My longing look Will go toward you."

Un Canadien Errant Antoine Gérin-Lajoie 1842.

Then Lemon strummed this old traditional lullaby for children, danced by the individuals he named. Faolan started it out by standing outside Caitlín's door.

162

"Au clair de la lune,
Mon ami Caitlín,
Prête-moi ta plume
Pour écrire un mot.
Ma chandelle est morte,
Je n'ai plus de feu.
Ouvre-moi ta porte
Pour l'amour de Dieu."

Au clair de la lune,
Caitlín répondit :
"Je n'ai pas de plume,
Je suis dans mon lit.
Va chez la voisine,
Je crois qu'elle y est,
Car dans sa cuisine
On bat le briquet."

Au clair de la lune,
S'en fut petit Faolan
Frappe chez la rousse.

Elle répond soudain:
—Qui frappe de la sorte?

Il dit à son tour:
—Ouvrez votre porte,
Pour le Dieu d'Amour.

Au clair de la lune,
On n'y voit qu'un peu.
On chercha la plume,
On chercha du feu.
En cherchant d'la sorte,
Je n'sais c'qu'on trouva;

"By the light of the moon,
My friend Caitlín,
Lend me your quill
To write a note.
My candle is dead,
I have no more fire.
Open your door for me
For the love of God."

By the light of the moon,
Caitlín replied:
"I don t have any pens,
I am in my bed
Go to the neighbor's,
I think she's there
Because in her kitchen
Someone is lighting the
fire."

By the light of the moon,
Went little Faolan
Knocks on the redhead's
door.

She suddenly responds:
—Who's knocking like
that?

He then replies:
– Open your door
for the God of Love!

By the light of the moon,
One could barely see.
The pen was looked for,
The light was looked for.
With all that looking

163

Mais je sais qu'la porte Sur eux se ferma.	I don't know what was found; But I do know that the door Shut itself on them.

The music stopped but Étienne tapped at Bridget's door anyway. "I can't sleep *avec* all this *désordre*," he said.

You're a red rosebud;
I'm the dirt in your garden—
Sink roots into me.

"Go back to bed, flapdoodle," said Bridget, and pulled a blanket over her head. "Song's over."

The next morning Lemon called a meeting to discuss plans. Everyone dragged themselves in and sat sheepishly on the benches.

"Long night?" he asked but there was no response.

"I think we should go find this address," Aoife said finally. She handed him the old letter.

"Well this is clear enough if you breathe on it first and squint," he said. "138 St. James Avenue, Boston, Massachusetts, United States of America. That's right here, isn't it?"

But it wasn't exactly. In fact, it was out in the Boston Back Bay which was, of course, filled with water and crabs. This they were told later by the clerk at City Hall. But the Registrar of Deeds found something interesting. A man named G. Gross was filling in the bay with dirt from railroad construction and making his money by selling house lots. He was using the trains and newly

164

invented steam shovels. As he was filling in the streets he left the house basements hollowed out. 138 St. James Avenue had recently been deeded to one "Bridget O'Day" by her parents presumably, but only a small down payment was recorded. There was a handwritten note in the file that said the whole family had been killed during a "civil disturbance," a euphemism presumably for drunken street brawling. It also stated that the property would escheat to the Commonwealth of Massachusetts after one year.

Lenna Ó Leannáin put his arm over Bridget as she wept softly. With a sombre face, he paid off the debt for considerably less than the amount written on the paper. Nevertheless, it took the rest of his cash. With a flourish, he handed over the deed to the girl who folded it carefully and placed it in her sack. "Now you won't be penniless," he said, "even if all you own is water and a few crabs." Bridget's tearful face betrayed the hint of a smile. Before they left the Courthouse Lemon thought to get Naturalization Papers for all of them to become US citizens. Even Aurora, born on the high seas with Caitlín Shaughnessy listed as mother, was now an American. This was in stark contrast to the thousands of Native Americans who did not receive citizenship until June 2, 1924.

Jewels

Back in their rooms, Lemon called another meeting. "Well, we need jobs now but the locals resent us Irish being willing to work for under a dollar a day. I'm seeing 'No Irish Need Apply' signs all over the city…"

Aoife cut him off. "Well then it's high time I sold my necklace. You only gave it to me for safekeeping anyway."

The first jeweller they approached indicated that it was not an emerald but a much less valuable garnet and with many specks bringing its value down. He offered a pitiful sum. Lemon perceived a speck in the merchants's eye as well and decided to take their business elsewhere. After several stops a tiny old man with a shaky hand and rimless glasses clinging to the end of his nose said, "This is a nice four carat green garnet called a demantoid. See how it plays with colour. It's splitting the light even better than a diamond. Indeed, it's one of the most precious of all gemstones."

"But what about the flaws in it?" Aoife asked.

"Those are horsetail inclusions," he said, "golden brown crystal threads of chrysotile. See how they radiate out from the centre in feathery golden threads, curved like horse tails. These actually make it much more valuable. I can sell this for quite a substantial sum." Aoife's mouth hung open. Lemon persuaded the jeweller to offer considerably more even than that, but there were many wealthy "Boston Brahmins" ready to make the old man a handsome profit.

Aoife persuaded Lemon to give her half the money and she bought many household items including a canary from the Hartz Mountains in Germany and naturally, her big brass bed. They could hardly get it all stuffed into her cubicle, but Faolan did help, even though the bird irritated him. Still, Aoife's eyes were heavy at the thought of losing the very jewel that gave her any tangible self-worth. She just wanted to lie down and take a nap so she told Faolan to leave her alone.

166

All the cubicle doors in the corridor looked the same and one day Jean entered Bridget's by mistake. He saw her spread out on her bed amidst an amazing array of jewellery and gold coinage. "*Pardonnez-moi!*" he gasped.

"Oh wait," she called. "Come in. You won't tell anyone, will you? I need this for my future."

"Your future looks bright indeed," he said. "Oh my, you even have several diamond engagement rings. Who are the lucky fellows?"

"They're from the coffin ship and their luck ran out. A shark ate them, in fact."

Jean didn't know what to say. He picked one up. "This is particularly nice. Do you think it would fit Caitlín?"

"I'm not marrying her," Bridget chuckled.

"But I may," said Jean, turning his head.

Bridget's mouth dropped open. "But you're—a priest!"

"No, I never was that in my heart," he said. "You know it to be true, and if I had this ring I could ask for hers. I'd pay you back."

"Oh no," Bridget said, "I'll consider it a wedding present to my dear Caitlín if she accepts. But never tell anyone where you got it, okay?"

"*D'accord.*"

"And you have to go to a proper minister to do the deed, okay?"

"*D'accord.*"

"And stop making so much noise late at night."

Jean Marie Delacroix left her room with a twinkle in his eye.

The Evangelist

There was an evangelist in town named Charles Phineas Haddon. Everyone just called him Reverend Finny. He was tall, stern and always wore black. The front half of his skull was completely bald but the rest was a luxurious growth of thick, wavy white hair, giving the illusion of riding in a stiff breeze. Not a man for light or frivolous conversation, his thundering voice brought countless into his tent every night and many to the Lord. In fact it grew into an old-fashioned revival. Jean started taking Caitlín there regularly and one evening they were so swept away by the spirit, an associate minister married them. There was no mention of his priesthood. Jean Marie Delacroix and Caitlín Shaughnessy—they just wanted to love and love every thing and every body. When Reverend Finny found out, he asked to see them and this became the first in a series of meetings. "Remedial-marital counselling," he called it. Immediately, he found their stories unique and engaging. They, in turn, clung to his every word, especially these: *"Do you not realize that the love the Father bestowed on the perfect Christ He now bestows on you?"*

"Guys, you just have to come hear this evangelist," Caitlín was bubbling at Lemon's next meeting. "He has this amazing voice that you can hear all the way in the last row. He says Christ loves us and we don't have to earn our salvation ourselves. And many other things. And his assistant evangelist married us right then and there," she added, flashing her ring.

There was stunned silence.

"Why so fast?" Bridget asked.

"Let's just say it needed to be done quickly to avoid appearance of sin."

Aoife and Faolan eyed each other. "You should have invited us," said Aoife.

"I just did," said Caitlín.

Aoife wrinkled her brow. "May we come tonight then?"

They all went and sat quietly on the back row of benches. There was a lot of clapping and standing and jumping and raising hands which made them feel like turtles on a log.

Then there was this loud and melodious hymn:

Am I a soldier of the cross,
A follower of the Lamb,
And shall I fear to own His cause,
Or blush to speak His Name?
Must I be carried to the skies
On flowery beds of ease,
While others fought to win the prize,
And sailed through bloody seas?
Are there no foes for me to face?
Must I not stem the flood?
Is this vile world a friend to grace,
To help me on to God?
Sure I must fight if I would reign;
Increase my courage, Lord.
I'll bear the toil, endure the pain,
Supported by Thy Word.
Thy saints in all this glorious war
Shall conquer, though they die;
They see the triumph from afar,
By faith's discerning eye.

When that illustrious day shall rise,
And all Thy armies shine
In robes of victory through the skies,
The glory shall be Thine.

It was stirring but none of them felt inclined to become soldiers of the cross or to receive Christ at the alter call. They had just finished sailing through their own bloody seas, thank you very much. Afterwards Caitlín led them up front anyway, but continued through a tiny door behind the stage. "These are my friends," she announced.

"Were you all on the coffin ship *Agnes Dei*?" Reverend Finny asked.

"Yes, except for Jean here and his boy Étienne," Aoife said. "I'm afraid *Agnes* drove us away from the merciful Lord you boast about."

The man looked at her kindly. "*A dark cloud is no sign that the sun has lost his light ; and dark black convictions are no arguments that God has laid aside His mercy. I have learned to kiss the wave that throws me against the Rock of Ages.*

"*An old Puritan once said, 'A full wind is not so favourable to a ship when it is fully fair as a side wind. It is strange that when a wind blows in an exact direction to blow a ship into port, she will not go near so well as if she had a cross wind sideways upon her. The mariners say that when the wind blows exactly fair it only fills a part of the sails, and it can not reach the sails that are ahead, because the sail, bellying out with the wind, prevents the wind from reaching that which is further ahead. But when the wind sweeps sideways, then every sail is full, and she is driven on swiftly in her course with the full force of the wind. Ah ! There is nothing like a side wind to drive God's people to heaven. A fair*

170

wind only fills part of their sails ; that is, fills their joy, fills their delight ; but the side wind fills them all ; it fills their caution, fills their prayerfulness, fills every part of the spiritual man, and so the ship speeds onward toward its haven.' It is with this design that God sends affliction, to chasten us on account of our transgressions. Affliction and then mercy through it."

You will tell his people how to find salvation through forgiveness of their sins. Because of God's tender mercy, the morning light from heaven is about to break upon us, to give light to those who sit in darkness and in the shadow of death, and to guide us to the path of peace.
                        Luke 1:77-79

As he was reading the Scripture, Caitlín reached into her bag and brought out the Irish Bible covered in sharkskin. She extended it to Aoife who just made a face and brushed it aside.

"*Half our fears arise from neglect of the Bible,*" the preacher said.

"When God turned away," said Lemon, "we had to rely on our own knowledge and inventions to survive. And survive we did."

The preacher stared at their Bible. "*Nobody ever outgrows Scripture. The book widens and deepens with our years. Wisdom is the right use of knowledge. To know is not to be wise. Many men know a great deal, and are all the greater fools for it. There is no fool so great a fool as a knowing fool. But to know how to use knowledge is to have wisdom.*"

So we have not stopped praying for you since we first heard about you. We ask God to give you complete knowledge of his will and to give you spiritual wisdom and understanding.
                                        Colossians 1:9

Lemon fingered his beard and stroked Scannalan's forehead.

"You don't know what we've been through," said Bridget. "We're weeds at sea tossed in a trash line."

Reverend Finny frowned. "Little one, *what if others suffer shipwreck, yet none that sail with Jesus have ever been stranded yet.*"

So you see, the Lord knows how to rescue godly people from their trials, even while keeping the wicked under punishment until the day of final judgment.
                                        2nd Peter 2:9

Then he looked deep into her eyes, *"Trials teach us what we are ; they dig up the soil, and let us see what we are made of."*

"I must be pretty thin clay then," Bridget said. *"If the Lord is with us, why has all this happened to us? And where are all the miracles our ancestors told us about? ...Now the Lord has abandoned us."* Judges 6:13

He took her young hand in his two old ones.

"You have trials, but you have a treasure as well, don't you? *Men know not the gold which lies in the mine of Christ Jesus, or surely they would dig in it night and day. They have not yet discovered the pearl of great price, or they would have sold their all to buy the field wherein it lies.*"

172

Again, the Kingdom of Heaven is like a merchant on the lookout for choice pearls. When he discovered a pearl of great value, he sold everything he owned and bought it!
Matthew 13:45-47

"You know the verse that brought me over to Christ?" Reverend Finny continued. "I was on my way to church one Sunday but a driving snowstorm steered me to a tiny chapel on a side street. Their pastor was snowbound so a skinny, simple shoemaker went up to the pulpit to give a message. He knew nothing else to say but his text: Isaiah 45:22 – *Let all the world look to me for salvation! For I am God; there is no other.* 'You just have to look;' he said, 'you don't have to lift a finger or a foot. A child can do it. Look to Christ—dead and buried yet risen and sitting at the right hand of God. Young man just look and stop looking so miserable.' Oh that somebody had told me this before. Trust Christ and you shall be saved simply by **looking** to Jesus. I had been delivered from despair."

How ironic that perhaps the most influential preacher who ever lived was saved through the sermon of a common shoemaker. What impact that little man had on the world one snowy morning. And how marvellous for God to bring glory to his name in such a manner. The preacher later said, *"While others are congratulating themselves, I have to sit humbly at the foot of the cross and marvel that I'm saved at all."*

Étienne was standing behind them, grouped around the evangelist. As it was time to leave, each departed wearing a different face—one blank, one straight, one sad, one fallen, one ashen, one of two minds. But the last to turn away had tears running over its cheeks. Over its sin. Inside was a dead heart spilling out and being replaced with a live one. A new birth. Not of his own making. But no one noticed as they shuffled through the tent flap and down the road. No one except Étienne himself that is—and a thousand angels. It was late when they got to their rooms so the boy tried to say goodnight to Bridget then fell asleep alone with his thoughts—but they were not of the girl.

The next day they all looked for jobs but still there were none. The money was running out yet somehow Lemon managed to bring in a sack of food every afternoon. After they'd eaten, Aoife said, "Let's go back to the tent meeting."

They walked in to the sound of serious singing:

When I survey the wondrous cross
On which the Prince of glory died,
My richest gain I count but loss,
And pour contempt on all my pride.

Forbid it, Lord, that I should boast,
Save in the death of Christ my God!
All the vain things that charm me most,
I sacrifice them to His blood.

See from His head, His hands, His feet,
Sorrow and love flow mingled down!
Did e'er such love and sorrow meet,
Or thorns compose so rich a crown?

Were the whole realm of nature mine,
That were a present far too small;

Love so amazing, so divine,
Demands my soul, my life, my all.

Aoife had pondered the darkness in her heart before. "I have something to tell you," she told the evangelist after the singing. It comes from my blackest days burying bodies, both at sea and on shore."

Fever, seizures, fear,
God sings dying sheep to sleep—
Counts tears in bottles.

Reverend Finny replied:

Pray against evil.
But we are evil,
But for Christ.

"But why is there evil and why must it touch me so hard?" Aoife asked.

"Evil is from man and not God," he replied, "and *beware of no man more than of yourself; we carry our worst enemies within us.*"

The human heart is the most deceitful of all things, and desperately wicked.
Jeremiah 17:9

"Oh, come, Divine Physician, and bind up every broken bone. Come with Thy sacred nard which Thou hast compounded of Thine own heart's blood, and lay it home to the wounded conscience and let it feel its power. Oh ! Give peace to those

whose conscience is like the troubled sea which cannot rest."

"Are you saying we are evil inside?" Caitlín asked.

The Reverend replied:

For everyone has sinned; we all fall short of God's glorious standard.
Romans 3:23

For the wages of sin is death, but the free gift of God is eternal life through Christ Jesus our Lord.
Romans 6:23

"All the goodness I have within me is totally from the Lord alone," he said. *"When I sin, it is from me and is done on my own, but when I act righteously, it is wholly and completely of God. Lord Jesus, we come just as we are ; this is how we came at first, and this is how we come still, with all our failures, with all our transgressions, with all and everything that is what it ought not to be, we come to Thee."*

"But I am already a good Catholic," Caitlín said.

The reverend pressed his lips together. "I can see that by the fine silver and gold crucifix you're wearing. But *there are some people who need to wear a label round their necks to show that they are Christians at all, or else we might mistake them for sinners, their actions are so like those of the ungodly.* You wear yours as a decoration on your front; Christ wore his on his back."

Caitlín bowed her head and thought of her sin-baby tossed overboard in a soup bowl. She ran her fingers through her hair. "A thistle is still a weed, no matter how pretty its flower."

The evangelist wiped his bald forehead.

He will not crush the weakest reed or put out a flickering candle.
Isaiah 42:3

"A sinner is spiritually dead; he *can no more repent and believe without the Holy Spirit's aid than he can create a world. By perseverance the snail reached the ark. Saving faith is an immediate relation to Christ, accepting, receiving, resting upon Him alone, for justification, sanctification, and eternal life by virtue of God's grace.*"

Lemon cleared his throat and perched stiffly at the end of his chair. "The blind go in circles to avoid running into corners."

Reverend Finny looked at him and said:

Christ emptied Himself
By taking the form of a servant.
Satan filled himself
By taking the form of a serpent.
How 'bout them apples!

Then his gaze flittered between Aoife and Caitlín who were sitting across from him holding hands. "*I believe that nothing happens apart from divine determination and decree.*"

Even before he made the world, God loved us and chose us in Christ to be holy and without fault in his eyes. God decided in advance to adopt us into his own family by bringing us to himself through

Jesus Christ. This is what he wanted to do, and it gave him great pleasure.
Ephesians 1:4-5

"We shall never be able to escape from the doctrine of divine predestination - the doctrine that God has foreordained certain people unto eternal life."

"Eternal life?" Bridget piped up. Her eyes appeared a bit dark and sunken. "I can barely stand being so poor and crappy in this one."

"It is not how much we have, but how much we enjoy, that makes happiness. You know this, Bridget. *Anxiety does not empty tomorrow of its sorrows, but only empties today of its strength."*

Jesus replied, "I tell you the truth, unless you are born again, you cannot see the Kingdom of God."
John 3:3

Lemon wagged a gnarly finger in his face. "Save your breath for preaching, Parson, you have more chance of proselytizing wee Scannalan here than ever an old Irish Pooka like me."

On that note they departed but later Caitlín crept into Aoife's room and into bed with her. Aoife muttered into her ear, "Are you troubled? It's okay; you may snuggle with me. In the workhouse I had to sleep with another Catholic girl, named Saoirse. It was okay but she would not come away with us because she was pregnant by evil. Like you. Now I fear we are both lost." Tears ran between their cheeks as they embraced.

"Can we just *look* for Jesus right here? The real one," Caitlín whispered. "That's our sin—we turned our backs on him."

My sin against God,
My dear Father in heaven,
Is sin against love.

So they closed their eyes and just looked. Looked and looked, silently until all there was— was looking—until the only thing that moved was the Holy Spirit. That proved to be enough; it became everything; they fell hard into him forever. And for the first time in their lives experienced being truly loved from the inside out. Caitlín purred, "Now I will never have to experience for myself just how much my sin cost Jesus on the cross." Aoife's tear ran into her hair.

The next morning they woke up together. "Why don't you take back your Bible?" said Caitlín.

Aoife, a changed person, stroked it fondly. "Thank you for keeping it for me, Caitlín. I guess it's like its cover. Rub it the wrong way and it becomes prickly; stroke it right and it's the smoothest thing around." She opened it in the middle and fell into Psalm 27:1.

The Lord is my light and my salvation—so why should I be afraid? The Lord is my fortress, protecting me from danger, so why should I tremble?

They stared at each other. So why were they still shaking? Could it be their hearts were still divided? Even after all this? At this point Bridget walked in—looking more mature with each passing day. Aoife held her head in both hands and with noses almost touching…

In coming of age,
From whom do you move away?
Never God, I pray.

Chapter 8

A Athair inmain, cluinte mo núall-sa:
mithig (mo-núarán!) lasin trúagán trúag-sa.
A Chríst mo chride, cip ed dom-aire,
a Flaith na n-uile, rop tú mo baile.

Beloved Father, hear, hear my lamentations.
Timely is the cry of woe
of this miserable wretch.
O heart of my heart, whatever befall me,
O ruler of all, be thou my vision.

The Conestoga

The Conestoga was a heavy, covered wagon used in the east to transport cargo. It was named for a local Indian tribe before its extermination. The lumbering monstrosity had upturned ends, like a ship, to keep cargo from spilling out. Graceful, but the ride was too bumpy to sit inside. So all Lenna Ó Leannáin's tribe walked alongside. Their amassed cargo from Boston, including the brass bed and canary, was stowed under the distinctive, sloping canvas tarp. They walked on the right side of the road with the teamster who controlled six muscular oxen with verbal commands and whipcracks. Also, he worked the brake handle protruding from the left side between the two wheels there. Driving on the right thus, it took them two weeks to get to Albany. Ambling along gave Lemon ample time for his poem.

18
This trust was Poem's covenant,
Made by Him alone;
He chose one Race called Racer great,
A nation as His own.
This Racer raised so many sons,
As stars they soon would be;
'Till Worthy One of purest blood,
Securely rescued thee.
And Racer too was promised land,
Much more than dust and sand;
Of Milk and honey, rain and grain,
And all from Love's own hand.
A torchlight walked through death parts planned,
As Glare pot fumed in vain.

The Erie Canal

Just north at Troy they boarded a succession of boats to ply the Mohawk River, then the Erie Canal all the way to Buffalo, situated on Lake Erie. This manmade waterway was forty feet wide and four feet deep with one towpath usually on the north side. Lemon procured them an interesting canal boat christened *Flat-Bottomed Bertha*. It was fourteen feet wide and seventy-four long, with a three and a half foot draft. A family of four lived on it: father, mother, and two boys, twelve and sixteen. Four

mules as well, named Sal, Hal, Gal, and Pal.
Charles Darwin had once noted recently that the
mule was surprising because it had more reason,
memory, obstinacy, sociability, muscular
endurance, and longevity than either of its parents.
But it was sterile and didn't exactly fit in with his
new theory of evolution. The canal boat operators
valued it for the size and ground-covering ability of
its horse mother and the endurance and disposition
of the donkey father. It was also stronger, hardier,
and required less food than a horse of similar size.
Two were harnessed to pull the boat while the other
pair rested and ate hay in a stable in the bow. One
boy was assigned to each team and he drove them
for six hour shifts. Getting a stubborn mule into the
boat was often an adventure. Occasionally a block-
and-tackle and another mule was needed to pull it
over the slightly arched hoss-bridge. Also, the
mules smelled but not as bad as the boys. Even
Scannalan noticed that.

The youngsters were rough in looks and
language. They enjoyed teasing Bridget and
watching her face glow red. She attracted them like
flies to sugar. One tried to get her to ride a mule but
she turned up her nose. They teased her with a giant
"New World mosquito." It was only a harmless
jinny-spinner. Nevertheless, crane-flies are scary
when thrust in a person's face. To get away, she
consented to come up on the flat roof with the
younger boy. They watched the green canal water
receding in their wake.

"You know, you're nothing but a bee drawn to
a flame," the boy said.

184

"Moth," the girl said.

"Okay, a bee drawn to a moth." He then pointed out some mallards diving in a nearby pond.

"Arsefeet," she said.

He pretended to be shocked at such language but then said a few things that made her blush. Of late, she'd been trying to control how pink her ears glowed. "Duck!" he shouted, stepping in front of her.

"Yes, I know," she said, "a mallard duck."

Suddenly his eyes grew large and he opened his arms wide.

"Why you doing that?" she asked.

"Because you about to fall into my ever-lovin' arms! A bee to a moth."

Just then the boat passed under a low bridge and it hit her squarely in the back. They were only going four miles per hour but that was enough to shove her into his arms and together they fell to the roof deck. His body cushioned her fall but she sprung up like a wet cat and gave him a big dose of some sailor-talk she'd picked up on the high seas. On her flight down the stairs she felt her ears turning again. Étienne looked on anxiously but she brushed him aside. She would smell like "mule-boy" for days, she feared.

To while away the hours perched atop the roof Lemon recited his epic poem to everyone—and no one.

19
Then Poem Love with His own hand,
Guided the Racer clan.
What many meant for evil only,
Love had a better plan.

185

Like a brother sold to bondage cruel,
A lowly household slave,
Becomes a boss of foreign lands,
His family to save.
Thus Racer knew not want or war,
And grew in sum and might,
Till yoked they were in servitude—
"Oh Love please make it right!"
So Poem plagued; the awful blight
Passed o'er the blood rescued.

"Paul wrote this wonderful passage in my Bible," Aoife said. "I think it's about us."

Can anything ever separate us from Christ's love? Does it mean he no longer loves us if we have trouble or calamity, or are persecuted, or hungry, or destitute, or in danger, or threatened with death? (As the Scriptures say, "For your sake we are killed every day; we are being slaughtered like sheep.") No, despite all these things, overwhelming victory is ours through Christ, who loved us.
And I am convinced that nothing can ever separate us from God's love. Neither death nor life, neither angels nor demons, neither our fears for today nor our worries about tomorrow—not even the powers of hell can separate us from God's love. No power in the sky above or in the earth below—indeed, nothing in all creation will ever be able to separate us from the love of God that is revealed in Christ Jesus our Lord.
Romans 8:35-39

But then she turned a few pages back to read about how Paul himself had suffered shipwreck and snakebite.

186

Once we were safe on shore, we learned that we were on the island of Malta. The people of the island were very kind to us. It was cold and rainy, so they built a fire on the shore to welcome us.

As Paul gathered an armful of sticks and was laying them on the fire, a poisonous snake, driven out by the heat, bit him on the hand. The people of the island saw it hanging from his hand and said to each other, "A murderer, no doubt! Though he escaped the sea, justice will not permit him to live." But Paul shook off the snake into the fire and was unharmed. The people waited for him to swell up or suddenly drop dead. But when they had waited a long time and saw that he wasn't harmed, they changed their minds and decided he was a god.

Acts 28:1-6

"Well Saint Paul was special because he was an apostle of Jesus Christ," Caitlín said.

"And we are special because we are his brides," Aoife replied. "Also saints."

"You have to be canonized to become a saint," said Jean.

"And dead," said Caitlín.

Aoife bristled. "Your saints are in heaven," she said, "the Bible's are on earth as his church. Anyone who has received Jesus Christ by faith is a saint."

"Okay, Saint Aoife," Caitlín said, "but I'd prefer not being shipwrecked or bitten by any poisonous snakes, if you please."

Aoife replied:

Don't worry about anything; instead, pray about everything. Tell God what you need, and thank him for all he has done.
                                    Philippians 4:6

Certainly there was little chance of shipwreck on the Erie Canal. Whenever the *Bertha* encountered another boat head-on, the one with the right of way stayed on the towpath side of the canal. The other steered carefully toward the heelpath side. The mule driver, or hoggee (HA-gee), of the privileged boat kept his towpath team near the canal-side edge of the path, while the hoggee of the other moved to the outside and stopped his team. His towline would fall slack into the water and sink to the bottom. The privileged team would step over the other boat's towline pulling their boat over the sunken line without stopping. When clear, the other boat's team would continue on its way. It was an intricate square-dance pull-by, usually performed quite elegantly. Bridget found a new respect for her hoggee boys.

Now the fancy packet boats carried only passengers and often at an illegal six miles an hour. But if caught, they could easily afford to pay the ten dollar fine. These boats were pulled by handsome horses and could be converted into elegant dining rooms and then sleeping quarters with fold-down bunks for forty some passengers. There were curtains down the middle to separate the sexes. Of course, the packet boats always claimed right-of-way. That is until Lenna Ó Leannáin began standing on *Bertha's* bow and directing traffic. He was wearing a purple cloak he'd bought in Boston which made him resemble Merlin the Magician. When he waved his shillelagh as a wand the *Flat-Arsed Bertha*, as he called her, yielded to no boat.

Along its 363 mile length, the Erie Canal needed to rise 566 feet up from Albany to Buffalo. To accomplish this, it used 72 locks scattered along the way. Each had huge watertight doors, called gates at both ends so boats could be raised or lowered. Agile Scannalan liked to show off by climbing up the stone side of the locks as the boat was lifted by the rising water level. Bridget was always afraid that he'd catch his tail and be crushed against the wall. "It would serve him right," thought Aoife.

One day, as they were approaching a lock, they had to wait a long time for a log raft coming the other way. It was made from timbers lashed together and being floated to market. It was slow, cumbersome, and its mules appeared bedraggled and overworked. Bridget watched as her two hoggee boys marched over to assist. They grabbed the stubborn mules by their noses and goaded them along with sticks to the groin. Well, their own hoggees took exception to this and soon a fight broke out—punching, swearing, and grappling on the ground. Something stirred in the girl at the sight of boys struggling with each other, nose to bloody nose in the dirt. Later she had to ask the Lord's forgiveness. Eventually it was all sorted out and life settled down again to the methodical clip clop of progress over the calm water. Yet Bridget still pondered the sin of fighting, and perhaps the even greater sin of watching it with such exhilaration. Her face flushed as she tended to a lip cut on one of her boys.

Aoife and Lemon were on the roof as the canal actually passed in the air over a river on an 800 foot aqueduct. "This is amazing," she said.

"It certainly is," said Lemon. "You know, this canal cost a thousand lives, seven million dollars, and eight years of digging, all with Irish hands. Did you know in the swamps they had to wait for winter and then dig channels in frozen water before shoring it up with wood? There was cholera, malaria, snakes and every manner of hardship. Still the thing is very profitable as evidenced by what they charge us to ride. Naturally, I get the price lowered by distracting some of the toll collectors along the way."

After 363 miles and ten days, twenty tons of clothing and furniture was unloaded in Buffalo by some burly longshoremen. Lemon would most miss the ornate side chair he had unpacked and sat in for days. Crafted in Boston with a high Gothic back of rich cherry, it made him look like a king. Also it was narrow enough to carry up to the roof. The others would miss some assorted wicker furniture they used to advantage. Clipper ships sailing from Asia were dumping their rattan packing material and an enterprising Bostonian was fabricating this into tables and chairs.

Of course, at trip's end, they carefully packed everything away again. As they said their goodbyes to the canal boat family, Bridget gave her hoggee boys a gift neatly wrapped in some of their home-school textbooks—which were nothing but old magazines. Walking away, she grinned watching them open it to find a box of "Snow Boy" washing powder.

Lake Erie

The next day Lenna Ó Leannáin was positively cock-a-hoop upon seeing "his" chair being loaded onto the lake steamer *SS P.G. Griffin*. She was a wooden sidewheel paddleboat carrying 326 immigrants to Toledo on Lake Erie with stops on the southern shore. Since they had half-price tickets, the Leannáin party of eight stayed on deck near the two tall, black smokestacks. The first order of business was the poem.

> 20
> The River Throner, his son dead,
> Let Racer go with gold;
> But Poem hardened his cold, black heart,
> To chase with wheels of old.
> Then Poem churned them in the sea,
> To free Racer to the Wild,
> To lead, to feed them, but they grumbled—
> Every man, woman and child.
> So Race went up, saw Poem Love,
> Who burned for eyes to see,
> And gave him ten Tabulations,
> Intended to keep them free.
> But utilized only to be,
> Fruitless works manipulations.

Aoife watched him from the corner of her eye. "Caitlín, I think he's talking about the Law of Moses." Her friend's expression remained blank. Aoife continued.

> **Lame? Walk in God's love.**
> **Blind? He's light for you to see.**
> **Law kills—Jesus heals.**

191

Bridget was tired of trying to avoid Étienne so she let him sit next to her, their legs dangling together over the side of the bridge connecting the two huge, churning paddlewheels. They sounded a rhythmic chug chug in the water like a lazy steam locomotive.

"But do you have to sit on my dress?" she said.

"Sorry, but it flows out so much we can't get close."

"No foolin', Sherlock," she said looking away. "Effey, is it fair that God hardens our hearts so we can't keep his commandments and then condemns us for not doing so?"

Her sister replied.

> **Law broken? Fine paid.**
> **God's children are forgiven—**
> **Just don't break church rules.**

Bridget squinted. She just didn't fathom how God works sometimes. After a few moments Lemon ambled up behind them. He was out lunting again with his dúidín pipe, all smoke and cape swirling together in the wind. "By the way, do yous know how those big paddlewheels work?"

"No," Aoife said, "but why do I have this feeling that you're going to tell us? Steam?"

"It's simple really. Steam powers the paddles but they must enter and exit the water almost vertically to be efficient. So there's an assembly of rods and levers set off-centre from the main drive-wheel— eccentric to tilt them properly. The way God drives us."

"Eccentric like you," said Bridget.

Lemon brandished his cape at her like a bat. "It's called feathering and this is all part of your

192

education my young Alanna. You'll need lots of facts to put in your book. And a lot more wisdom to put in your life."

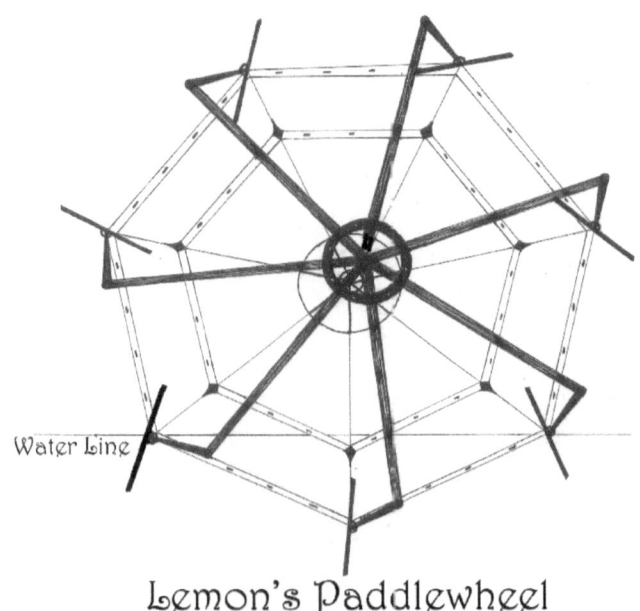

Water Line

Lemon's Paddlewheel

"And one more thing," he continued.

21
Poem so loved his chosen Race,
He gave them water cool;
And Glower Cakes new every day,
But they scoffed in ridicule.
So they wandered forty years away,
A generation gone,
With their precious Racer Poet gray,
From them in death withdrawn.
Then from the Wild, Love led them in,
To a land where honey flows;

But some were afraid and lonely,
To fight the giant foes;
But Poem victory bestows,
Through his mighty hand only.

The *Griffin* stopped at Fairport, Ohio and then was about two miles outbound when Lemon smelled smoke coming from one of the smokestacks near them.

"There's **supposed** to be smoke from a smokestack," Aoife grumbled, irritated at being jostled at four AM.

"Not from its base," Lemon said. "Wake the others. Move quietly. Bring nothing." He lowered the ship's small dingy into the water and they pulled away silently. After a few minutes they could see sparks around both stacks and general confusion on deck. The captain was steering full steam ahead toward land but this only served to fan the flames and soon the entire stern was engulfed. Eventually they hit a sandbar in eight feet of water, a half mile from land. In the melee most of the passengers were either burned to death, drowned instantly, or were pulled under by others who couldn't swim.

Lemon's little boat remained offshore in the darkness until things died down. Then they headed for a beach up the coast a ways. 250 people died that night but not all were accounted for straight away. At dawn, Aoife watched from the bushes as a few locals dug a mass grave and threw in 47 men, 24 women, and 25 children.

"I should go help them," she said.

"No," said Lemon, "they'll just ask how we survived the wreck and why we didn't help them."

"Why didn't we help them?" Aoife asked.

194

"Colleen girl, you are not everyone's saviour," he said. "But once again, I seem to be yours."

22
Promised land settled, enemies killed;
But not all, like Poem said.
He sent them leaders; they wanted Throners,
Like the pagans instead.
But most Throners were wicked,
So Poem sent Poets,
To display his glory and will,
So they would surely know it.
But they heard not, so he punished them,
To exile in foreign lands.
But Poem Love shepherded them there,
Safely in his sweet hands,
And the bloodline of the Worthy One stands,
In his sovereign care.

So they hid out until everything became quiet again. In the dark, they took stock of themselves. Everyone was present, safe, no injuries. But all else was lost. Their cargo from Boston was gone. All their clothes, except those on their backs, were burned. Caitlín clung to her baby and Aoife to her Bible. Bridget had been too sleepy and panicked to even bring her burlap bag of treasures. Jean Marie had lost all his flowing robes, ribbons, certificates and diplomas. Étienne had ripped his pants. Lemon, of course, had managed to save his cape, his shillelagh, his fiddle, and his entire bag of medicines and magic potions. And dear Scannalan, naturally.

23
Your weeping may last through the night,
But joy comes in the morning,
For Poem Love is your shepherd;
So fear no death or warning.
Be still and know that he is Love,
And you are wonderfully made;
This is the day that Love has given;
He shines, so be not afraid.
Let every psalm flow from your mouth,
Your hearts meditation,
Be pleasing in his sight, our rock,
Songs of adoration,
Broken hearted restoration,
The sheepfold of his flock.

The next night they spied the lights of another
steamer heading for Toledo. It was far down the
coast so they made preparations to row out to meet
it. As they passed the sandbar they encountered
several bloated bodies floating nearby. They were
white as ghosts with balloon faces and undulating
hair—men who had sunk straight to the bottom but
now were raised by putrefaction gases to dance on
the surface. Aoife told Faolan to stop looking at
them but Lemon asked him a question. "Why would
men sink so fast?"

"Look at their belts," Faolan said. Indeed their
bodies were tightly cinched in the middle by…"

"Row closer," Lemon said.

"No, we'll miss the steamer," Aoife said. They
drew alongside the macabre figures anyway.

"Money belts!" Jean said, "gold bars and coins
from Europe no doubt."

Sure enough, Faolan was able to cut away a
small fortune from the bobbing corpses before

rowing out to meet the steamship *Delaware*. Buying passage to Toledo would be no problem now.

Prairie Schooners

Toledo could have been a major metropolis but there was no proper canal ever built west to Chicago. The railroads were still a few years away so the Leannáin tribe decided to buy wagons with some of their gold. They would need them anyway for the ongoing trip westward and this way they didn't have to depend on others or waste money on tickets. In addition, they could replace all their goods in the city, even the brass bed and canary.

Lemon assumed he needed a pistol for the Wild West. In 1836 Samuel Colt had just patented the first mechanism that led to widespread use of the revolver. He got the idea while at sea, inspired by the capstan, which used a ratchet and pawl device. He used this in his guns to rotate the cylinder full of bullets. Lemon bought two of them.

Not to be outdone, the other men bought rifles or shotguns. Even Étienne, which amused Bridget. "Just the kick of that thing's gunna kill ya," she said. "Don't point it at me." He just smirked and held it close to his chest. It was rather taller than he.

Jean bought a prairie schooner, four strong mules, and three horses for his family—so Faolan did as well. Schooners were sturdy wagons with flat horizontal bodies—smaller and lighter than the Conestogas. They looked like sailing ships from a

ORW

distance—high, white sails, hulls four feet wide, and ten feet long, caulked and oiled for river crossings.

"Can I ride along?" Aoife asked. "And Bridget too?"

"If you behave yourselves," Faolan said. The three of them made a pretty picture sitting on the bench under the canvas bonnet. He looked stately in his cowboy hat, holding the reins with a sturdy pioneer girl at each arm. Granted, Aoife was on the frail side for Faolan and Bridget a bit short, but at least they were wearing prairie bonnets to match the wagon. The spare mules and horses trailed behind. Bridget found the ride quite rough.

"You know," she said, "an elf like me's got very little padding in the sit-down place." Faolan lolled his tongue out and retrieved pillows for both girls from one of the storage chests in back.

The Medicine Show

Lenna Ó Leannáin found not a prairie schooner, but a medicine wagon. It was nothing but a big, square box on large wooden-spoked wheels with metal rims, called "tires." It was small on the outside but remarkably ample for Lemon and all his paraphernalia on the inside. He also bought three wild mustangs. There was a sign crudely lettered on the corral fence: *For fast riders, we have fast horses. For slow riders, we have slow horses. For those who never have ridden, we have horses that have never been ridden.*

"Wild horses!" Aoife exclaimed. "Nobody can even get near them."

200

Lemon looked at her, "You know, wild horses all stand together in a field facing in the same direction. You know why?"

"Because they're waiting for you to tell them where to go next?"

"Pffft. They all face down wind so they can smell predators sneaking up behind but see anything coming from the front."

"Capture them from the side with a lasso," Faolan said.

"Oh, any fool can do that." Lemon said. "The lariat is made from such stiff rope the noose always stays open when thrown. It's nothing but tossing a hoop over a horse. But watch this." He pointed his shillelagh at one of the mustangs and started whispering something.

"No wait," Aoife said, "you're breaking its will."

Caitlín covered her mouth as Lemon stroked its nose. "Why such a long face?" he spoke to the horse, "I'm saving you from a life of wildness and fear. I use no ropes or spurs."

"Is this how we become Christians?" Caitlín asked.

"No," Aoife said, "we're not roped into it. We are all lost but God draws some of us irresistibly back to himself. Still it's up to us to accept him. Don't you remember what happened to us in bed that night?"

"Sister, that sounds like a contradiction," Caitlín said. "God is irresistible but we have a choice?"

"A contradiction only in our tiny human brains," Aoife said.

Lemon pointed his stick at another mustang, then turned to them. "Christ calls you to the suffering he endured. I bring you love and salvation from that pain. And also these three poor horses and a poem."

24
Poets of old foretold of the Word:
"Born of virgin, seed of Grace,
Kinsman redeemer, called Love's Son,
Suffering servant of Race.
A light to the world with healing signs,
Rejected cornerstone,
Son of Race, forsaken and pierced,
A great light on David's throne.
Preceded by a messenger,
Betrayed for thirty coins,
The innocent Passover lamb,
Stemmed from Abraham's loins.
A star, he's lifted high and joins
Resurrected! the great I AM."

The next day he borrowed a can of paint and lettered his new wagon: *Dr. Lancelot's Famous Magic Medicine Show*. "What a silly name," said Bridget, but it was quite apt, except for the "show" part. That was remedied in short order when Lemon "adopted" a delightful eight year-old girl. Or should I say, "abducted?" She was lost from her mother and quite adept at singing and dancing a "breakdown" on saloon tables—and the tops of medicine wagons they discovered. She was petit, perky, with blushing cheeks, brown eyes, and mischievous lips. She liked to sprinkle her light-red hair with cayenne pepper to catch the light playfully. It was parted in the middle, with bangs curled loosely and ringlets tumbling down the back of her neck. The lonely men of the Old West soon fell in love with her as a sweetheart doll. Their affections made her girlish features positively glow and she learned to tease them mercilessly with her dimpled chin, impish grins and winks. Lemon looked out for her quite carefully and also for all the silver dollars they gave her.

To her show talents Lemon added some trick shooting of his own. He learned to blast buttons off people's shirts and hit targets by ricocheting bullets off cast-iron frying pans. One day he placed his dear Lotta between himself and a whiskey bottle set up as a target behind her. Her lips quivered and hands shook as he flashed his cannon of a six-gun. But she stood bravely erect, only whimpering slightly as he loudly cocked the big barking iron. The crowd gasped and one man tried to intervene but the magician held him back with a wave of his gnarled wand. Then with his thumb, he shoved a slug into a chamber.

"Don't interfere," he said, "this takes an enormous amount of concentration and a young lady's life is at stake." Her face paled and her knees grew wobbly. Then, before they could stop him, he whipped the pistol around lightning fast like swatting a fly backhand on the wall. Midway, he let fly a shot which actually curved in mid-air around the child and shattered the bottle behind her. At this, Lotta fainted but miraculously recovered after a kiss on the forehead. There was wild applause. The act worked so well they repeated it every night. The fainting was such a good touch they decided to fake it from then on. Lemon never attempted to explain the physics of bending bullets to the girls. He said it was elvish in origin and he learned it from the writings of Fodbgen, a High King of Ireland.

204

It wasn't long before they painted red letters, "*Lotta ~ Lemon*"on the wagon and began selling refreshments. The medicine wagon had a mysterious chest with a seemingly endless supply of chopped ice inside.

"Never mind the lemonade," Bridget complained, "he spends all his time with that pop tart. He buys her lollies and fancy dresses just because she has pretty curls. I could sing and dance too, if I wanted. I could curl my hair. It's just because I'm so thin and small for my age. Where does she sleep in that little wagon anyway? All she does is cook and tidy up. She's his slave. I hate her."

Time passed on the monotonous trail but after they crossed into Illinois, Bridget joined the show as an enchanted elf. They cut her hair short, put a green leotard on her, with pointed shoes, and cellophane wings. Lemon taught her to blush and make her ears glow brighter in the dark. She began to look amazingly like a real elf.

"O my Lord," Lotta said, "why do we need her? She's just a pixie-faced ingénue. And way too skinny."

"O my Sweet," Lemon said, "That will only highlight how great you look. And she can't dance worth a plug nickel."

"A plug what?" Lotta asked.

"It's a one cent coin with the silver centre plug knocked out. Makes it worthless. Don't accept any of them from the men."

Scannalan was also in the show billed as an Irish sewer rat but everyone in these parts knew a possum when they saw one. But no one in the Wild

West towns, it seemed, had ever heard a poem like Lemon's.

25
Poem Love told his Poet: Go,
To a wicked city, cry,
"Hear my Song; turn your hearts,
Else you will surely die."
But Poet hated his enemy,
And sailed the other way,
In storm, but a fish swallowed him safe,
To cry another day.
So the town did all sing Poem's Song,
But the Poet still was sad.
So Poem grew a shade plant slim,
Which died and made him mad.
Such compassion for self, Poet had!
But Love's went well beyond him.

Along the way Lemon collected massasauga rattlesnakes to milk for his antivenin collection and other potions. To do this he would make them bite the rims of glasses covered with stretched lizard skins. The thick yellow venom would drain ominously down the sides. He kept the snakes in cages nailed to the outside of his wagon—along with a few assorted scorpions, centipedes, and tarantulas—to ward off burglars and fascinate young boys for ten cents. Soon he had so many creatures he started using them in his show. He would place a critter on the shoulder of each of his girls. "Now hold very still," he'd say. "They only strike at movement." Then he'd take twenty paces back and with two pistols shoot both off them simultaneously. Or else he'd fan one pistol with the same result. To fan he would hold down the trigger with one hand and repeatedly bang the hammer with the side of the other. As a finale, he'd fire a spider off both shoulders of a girl simultaneously with "one shot." First he'd pull the hammer back to cock the gun. Then, when she was ready, he'd release the hammer with the trigger and right after the hammer fell he'd fan off a second round. The report sounded like a single shot but in fact two spiders disappeared from the bare skin. It worked so well the girls had to stage being weak kneed and collapsing to the ground afterwards. Their fame quickly spread and the public began paying liberally to see such a spectacle. With his piles of cash Lemon took to poker gambling whenever he could and soon learned not to win too much on any given night—so as not to be branded a cheat. Still, he could always draw to an inside straight as if he knew what card would be dealt. His secret was not in the cards.

He loved to cry, "Wagons Ho!" The little train of three wagons skirted around the newly incorporated city of Chicago (which means garlic) and headed up into the new Territory of Wisconsin (which means red rock). White men of that time often took Indian terms to name things and Indians took White names to call themselves. The wagon train then came across some lead miners and they were tempted to settle in the area until they discovered they would have to shelter in holes dug into the ground.

"I want to be a farmer, not a badger," Faolan said.

Indian Attack

Travelling further north they encountered a chief and his queen and their two pack mules. The gentleman introduced himself as Red Bird, a medicine man of the local Winnebago tribe. His lady, Red Wing, dressed all in leather, never spoke but managed to sell Lemon twenty pairs of nice beaded moccasins anyway. In exchange for numerous tribal remedies wrapped in bark and many magnificent bald eagle feathers, the white man gave them several cases of whiskey, Étienne's rifle, …and a wee dose of his poetry.

> 26
> All Racer was captured by Throner 'Jerksies,'
> Who gave a party squirrely;
> His queen "V" wouldn't dance nude for them,
> So he queened one not so churly.
> Her cousin Mo was a Racer too,
> Not bowing to Hambone boss;
> So Hambone built a gallows for slaughter,
> And Racer'd be a total loss.
> Now cousin Mo had squealed to Jerksies,
> "How to fete a friend?" Jerk asked Ham;
> "A parade of honour," he replied surely,
> "Ham do that for Mo; stop your scam."
> Racer fights back, gets out of a jam,
> All through Jerk's Racer girly.

As they were leaving, Red Bird seemed quite fascinated with Lemon's wagon. So Lemon showed him the inside.

"Inconceivable," the Indian said in his native Hocak, "you have ample room for everything you need to live in there, even a bed and a squaw. You can travel everywhere without resorting to hotels or restaurants. Ingenious use of space. It's like you're always on vacation."

"Mister Big Bird," Bridget called from the back of her wagon, "What are you going to do with all that whiskey?"

"Small sparrow," he answered, "we use it to kill the pain."

"What pain?" But they had pulled away before he could speak.

Ambling along, Lenna Ó Leannáin did think of his life as one big holiday. He was free and lacked for nothing: money, companionship, adventure. Maid service. So he decided to change the name on the side of his wagon:

Doc Holliday's Winnebago Medicine Show

Inside on shelves were arrayed every sort of remedy known to man and more than a few that did more harm than good. There were countless bottles of what he called "Cocaine-Kola-Nut Wine" which in time he shortened to "Coca-Cola." He claimed it cured indigestion, nervousness, headaches, and impotence. Also there was another refreshment beverage, a lemon soft drink containing the mood stabilizer lithium citrate. He called it "Lemon-up." The biggest bottle he had contained laudanum, a 10 percent opium tincture in alcohol. He mixed it with brandy, mercury, turpentine, ether, and chloroform to make "Lemon-down" for supressing cough, diarrhoea, and pain. He sometimes added beef fat and labelled it as "Snake Oil" to smooth wrinkles, remove stains, and cure rashes. When Lotta came along he tossed in some of her cayenne pepper for good measure. He called that "Doctor Pepper." But of course, the best medicine was Lotta herself.

During each show Lemon would stand on an old wooden soapbox to give his sales spiel. He made liberal use of his cape and shillelagh. Étienne was placed in the audience as a shill to testify from personal experience as to the effectiveness of the products.

The Circuit Rider

During his ministry, circuit rider Jefferson Obadiah Cartwright rode over 200,000 miles on horseback. He preached over 50,000 sermons and wrote over 500 hymns. Many are still being sung today, but without all the verses. In his early years he was assigned a route in Wisconsin Territory to minister to settlers and plant little churches along the path. Regardless of storm or blazing sun he was always on track as a black-clad herald of Light. His hat and Bible were jet black. His saddlebags carried one change of clothes and a notebook in which he penned copious sermon ideas. But no food. He was fed and housed by people along the way, even Indians, who considered him a shaman.

As it happened, he met another shaman of sorts on the road. Lenna Ó Leannáin. In conversation, they steered apprehensively clear of each other but Aoife gave him a nice hot dinner of turkey and wild rice, a local Indian delicacy. As Aoife and Bridget were washing the dishes in the stream, he and Faolan sat around the fire drinking coffee. The preacher was licensed as an exhorter so he brought out his big, black King James and exhorted from Mark 7:9.

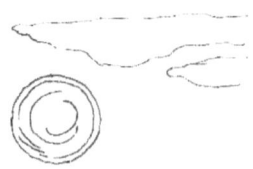

Full well ye reject the commandment of God, that ye may keep your own tradition.

"You honor Jesus with your lips but your heart is far away from him."

"I've been hearing so much about Jesus from these girls," Faolan said. "My head is spinning. One thing I just don't understand is what Aoife calls 'ejection.' She says that God chooses in advance who will be saved and who he will reject. She finds it all over the Bible but I don't like it. It just doesn't seem right or fair."

"Election," the circuit rider said, "the term is 'election.' I've heard a lot of people say it's not fair, so can I ask you a question? How would you do it if you were God? What would be more right and fair?"

"Well, I never would choose in advance who would live and who would die. I would give everyone an equal chance to be saved. I'd make sure every person who ever lived had opportunity to hear the gospel and have a fair chance to make a choice. And without me deciding their fate before they're born."

"Yes indeed, but you being God, you would be omniscient, all-knowing, right?"

"Well yeah. Of course," Faolan admitted.

"Then you'd already know every person's eternal fate before you created them. So by creating them you'd be sending them to either heaven or hell."

Faolan scratched his head roughly as if trying to harvest thoughts from his hair. "I guess my real question is: Why does God choose to save some people, but not others? Why doesn't he just save everybody?"

The preacher paused. "I asked that question for a long time myself. And the answer didn't come from some highfalutin theology but from one basic truth everyone knows. We're all sinners and the punishment for that is death. Therefore, we all deserve judgment for our sinfulness. Yes?

"Yeah."

"And we all need Jesus because without him as saviour we have no hope. Am I right?"

"Of course."

"We all deserve hell. It's a tough thing to say, but admitting this is necessary to accept Jesus' death on the cross that makes amends for our sin and saves us from this terrible fate. So if every single one of us deserves God's judgment, we shouldn't get hung up on the question, 'Why doesn't God save everyone?' The question that should really boggle our minds is: 'Why does God save anyone?'"

"Could he save even me?" Faolan asked.

The preacher looked directly into his steely eyes. "Well, that's the crux of the matter, isn't it? The crux, or cross is the heart of it. Where is yours? Just ask him and find out. You won't be disappointed. God is love."

Faolan lingered a long time over a sip of coffee. "I think I just did," he said. One sip was all he needed.

"Would you like to pray out loud?"

"Jesus God in heaven," the sailor began, wind filling his sails, "I'm sorry for stealing fish and running away from the ship. And please forgive me for only being nice to Aoife when the wind blows me into her lee shore. For otherwise ignoring her and having wishful thoughts about other beaches." He hung his head. "And most of all, would you please moor me fast to your own heart, even though I've sailed past it all my life? If it's not too late or too much trouble."

It wasn't and another soul found safe harbour. Never too late, never to leave.

I tell you that in the same way, there will be more joy in heaven over one sinner who repents than over ninety-nine righteous persons who need no repentance.

Luke 15:7 (NASB)

The circuit rider led the new believer in this song:

Our God, our help in ages past,
Our hope for years to come,
Our shelter from the stormy blast,
And our eternal home.

Under the shadow of Thy throne
Thy saints have dwelt secure;
Sufficient is Thine arm alone,
And our defense is sure.

Before the hills in order stood,
Or earth received her frame,
From everlasting Thou art God,
To endless years the same.

Thy Word commands our flesh to dust,
"Return, ye sons of men:"
All nations rose from earth at first,
And turn to earth again.

A thousand ages in Thy sight
Are like an evening gone:
Short as the watch that ends the night
Before the rising sun.

The busy tribes of flesh and blood,
With all their lives and cares,
Are carried downwards by the flood,
And lost in following years.

Time, like an ever rolling stream,
Bears all its sons away;
They fly, forgotten, as a dream
Dies at the opening day.

Like flowery fields the nations stand
Pleased with the morning light;
The flowers beneath the mower's hand
Lie withering ere 'tis night.

Our God, our help in ages past,
Our hope for years to come,
Be Thou our guard while troubles last,
And our eternal home.

Aoife returned with clean dishes to find her Faolan spotless as well. His face was shining.

If our death is just,
Then Mercy may choose to save,
Whomever it wills.

He did. Now they could be equally yoked, she thought, and never too soon, to her thinking.

The Third Commandment—
You've taken God's holy name;
Don't wear it in vain.

The Log Cabin

Not long after the circuit rider pulled away, the three wagons happened upon a quaint covered bridge over a small stream they took to calling River Snake. The bridge was a charming wood structure with a shake roof and red painted boards on its sides. There were three small windows on each side, and at each end the embankment had been built up impressively with rocks and cement. There were flowering meadows all around and stands of old oaks and conifers. The wind playing in their branches resonated reminiscent of the ocean. The field responded in gentle waves—bobbing colourful wildflowers. Nearby swelled an inviting grassy knoll.

"Jean, can you picture a log cabin up there?" Caitlín asked.

"With a stone chimney and smoke swirling a sweet fragrance up to the Lord," her husband replied.

Next day, they journeyed back to the little town and Lemon purchased the whole 320 acre parcel for them, covered bridge and all. For good measure, he added a horse drawn walking plow. It was a new kind, iron faced with steel saw blades. Also a brush harrow, a cutting sickle, and a flail.

Lemon had to explain the use of a flail. "It's for threshing—separates grains from their husks. It's simply two large sticks attached by a short chain; you swing one stick, causing the other, the

216

swipple, to strike a pile of grain, loosening the husks.

He also bought an ample supply of seedcorn and wheat seed to start them out. They came in burlap sacks not unlike Bridget's first dress.

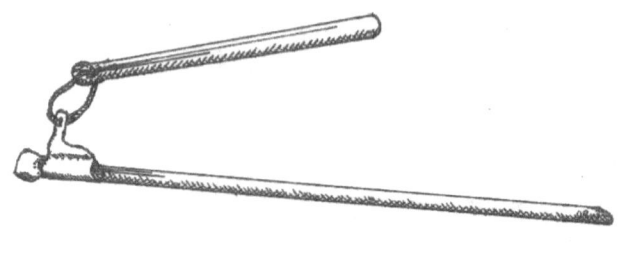

flail

"You will never lack for clothes for the baby, or curtains for the windows," she said.

Soon they were camping out on the grassy knoll and driving in stakes for the log cabin.

"This place will be our salvation, our redemption," Lemon said.

"Provided by God," Aoife said.

"No, provided by me, your counsellor," Lemon said. "Listen."

27
Word became Race, Song glorified,
In a Pet's used feeding tray—
So glowers sang but Glare so snarled,
He tried to eat him that day.
Yet Racers left their Pets and knelt,
At baby Worthy One;
Their salvation and redemption,
Had only just begun.
Then some Robeys brought gifts from the East,

But received more than fine gold,
From a Love that would never cease,
In tales forever retold—
Oh the wonderful counsellor of old,
And the Mighty Prince of Peace.

"Don't build on the top of the hill where the cold north wind blows," Jean said. "Come down off the crest a bit and dig into the south hillside."

"I want to have lots of windows and see everywhere," Caitlín said.

"Trust me, you won't by Christmastime," her husband replied.

Faolan shot a big bear the first day. They smoked most of the meat to eat later and scraped the hide to make two window coverings. Thin and greased, the skin became quite translucent to let in light but keep the cold out. Jean kept warning them to prepare for the change of season but the Irish folk never fully appreciated the urgency.

"It'll get *très froid* in these parts and the snow will cover your belt buckles. We need to lay in *beaucoup* food and firewood for a long winter."

Faolan was nothing short of mighty with an axe and the girls trimmed off the branches and bark of his fallen trees. Étienne used the mules and chains like a hoggee to haul the thick, straight timber to the building site.

Soon they were adopted by a young orphaned racoon they christened Puck. "A good fellow, shrewd and knavish sprite," said Lemon. Scannalan didn't think he was all that shrewd or spriteful. More comical than cute and certainly not as handsome as himself. They steered well clear of each other.

The cabin was built in three ten-foot sections. First they hauled four enormous flat stones up from the creek, then smaller ones to build a firebox. Each flat stone became a foundation corner.

"Christ has become my cornerstone," Caitlín remarked as they were placing the first one in the dirt. "Everything in my life is built in reference to this rock."

"Face the door and windows to the south," Lemon said, "the sun is our sustainer, not some rock." Caitlín frowned.

They cut deep notches at the ends of each log to fit them together as they stacked the walls. The space between the logs was chinked with a mixture of mud and dry grass. Then they constructed a sloping roof of split logs and covered it with several layers of birch bark. On top of this came thick sod from the original foundation.

"Make the rafters strong," Jean said, "the snow load will be tremendous by February."

The fireplace was built of mud and fieldstone but the chimney was wood lined with clay. It tilted away from the house and was held up by poles on the outside. The dirt floor was then packed hard and smooth. Finally a wooden door was attached with leather hinges and a steel bolt from Toledo.

"When the house was completed and the brass bed, canary and everything else was inside, there was hardly room to move. As they were huddling around the new fireplace, Aoife brought out her Bible to read but Lemon piped up first.

28
Poem so loved the world, he gave,
His precious holy Word,
Who is the way. The truth, the life;

219

All else is quite absurd.
"You must be born again," says Word,
"To enter my realm of peace;
Blessed are you who hunger and thirst,
For righteousness to increase.
And when others persecute you,
Because you follow me,
Be not anxious about tomorrow;
I make you healed and free,
By hanging dead upon a tree,
Atoning your sin and sorrow."

Caitlín remarked, "I don't mean to be anxious but we need to start work on another house for you guys." The swirling smoke reminded Aoife of the famine cottage when she had no home of her own, and of the times she would read her Bible to Bridget.

"It's November already," Jean said, "and we still need more food and firewood. Not to mention an animal shelter."

"Yes," pronounced Lemon, "it looks like we'll all have to winter in this wee shack. Let's store most of our things in the wagons until spring."

"But not food; critters will get it," Jean said.

Aoife said, "I think we should pray and thank God for this house which will save us from the coming weather."

"God didn't give you this cabin," Lemon said, "I did. For Christmas, God will be giving you hungry wolves, wild cougars, and ever more irritated spiders in from the cold."

"No," Aoife said, "wasn't it God who saved us from the burning ship and the cholera epidemic?"

"Do recall the facts, my girl," Lemon replied. "Did God arrange for a train ride to Boston or did he lower a lifeboat into Lake Erie?"

"I think he did," Aoife said, just under her breath.

> **Your leaves blow against**
> **My sensibility fence—**
> **Frisky in the fall.**

Wintering in the cramped quarters was like being too many bees in a hive. Especially with two queens. Blankets were hung to divide the cabin into four zones. Half was a common area to cook, eat and sit by the fire. The rest was divided into thirds for group sleeping—one for men, one for women, and one for Lemon and all his medicines and creatures which he said couldn't be allowed to freeze in his wagon. Lotta slept at his feet but Scannalan preferred the warm rafters above the fire and away from the racoon. From time to time Jean would sneak in to visit Caitlín so Aoife and Bridget started sleeping in front of the fire—to keep it stoked during the night, they said. Really it was to look out for spider eye-shine in the rafters and alert Scannalan. Thereafter Jean moved in with his wife and little Aurora. One time, Faolan crept out to warm himself beside Aoife but Bridget poked him with the fireiron and hissed, "Not until you put a ring on it, Buster."

The next day Bridget and Lotta were alone by the fire. The cabin was surrounded by howling wind and wolves.

**Sleet pounds the rhythm;
Snowflakes dance its melody—
God writes the winter.**

They huddled under a single blanket. "You shouldn't be sleeping in there," Bridget said, glancing over at Lemon's curtain.

Lotta's eyes grew large. "My place is at the feet of my saviour."

"He's my saviour too," said Bridget, "but I don't sleep anydogwhere near him."

By Christmas the sinful randiness was getting so bad Lemon put a dash of saltpetre in the stew pot each night and a pinch of bromide in the morning tea kettle. Another remedy for cabin fever proved to be an old hornpipe he'd brought from *Agnes*, a penny whistle from an Illinois peddler, and of course his trusty fiddle. In addition, Étienne cut a fairly nice pan flute from river reeds. Eventually, all joined in what they called "the sassy snowbound jig." Lotta pounded out a rhythm using fiddlesticks on Lemon's strings as he bowed them. It was foolishness that bordered on insanity, an awful noise only God could enjoy. Even the crazy canary was chiming in. Puck scampered wildly between the flailing feet but Scannalan just peered down sideways from the safety of his rafter—as if from Mount Sinai. Then all of a sudden, a calmer spirit descended on them and they all joined hands in this:

Joy to the world, the Lord is come!
Let earth receive her King;
Let every heart prepare Him room,
And heaven and nature sing,
And heaven and nature sing,

And heaven, and heaven, and nature sing.

Joy to the earth, the Savior reigns!
Let men their songs employ;
While fields and floods, rocks, hills and plains
Repeat the sounding joy,
Repeat the sounding joy,
Repeat, repeat, the sounding joy.

No more let sins and sorrows grow,
Nor thorns infest the ground;
He comes to make His blessings flow
Far as the curse is found,
Far as the curse is found,
Far as, far as, the curse is found.

He rules the world with truth and grace,
And makes the nations prove
The glories of His righteousness,
And wonders of His love,
And wonders of His love,
And wonders, wonders, of His love.

Following this came plenty of pious prayer and Bible reading as they pondered their fate as poor immigrants against the raw and relentless elements of the American wilderness.

Óir tá fios na smaointe a smaoinim do bhur dtaobh agam, adeir an Tiarna, smaointí síochána agus ní oilc, a thabhairt críche agus dóchais daoibh.
For I know the plans I have for you," says the Lord. "They are plans for good and not for disaster, to give you a future and a hope.
Jeremiah 29:11

224

Bridget reached over and stroked the Bible cover in Aoife's lap. "God certainly had interesting plans for our shark, didn't he," she said, "I just hope we all come to as just an end as he did. Come to think of it, I haven't spoken to God in so long I'm not sure he would recognize me."

"Oh, he would," Aoife said, "it's you who aren't seeing him at this point."

The creek was frozen all winter so any water had to be melted from snow. That meant very little for laundry or bathing and by January there was a certain lack of freshness about everyone. Until spring cleaning, the freshest body in the house would be that of the canary. But all remained healthy except Bridget who seemed to be losing weight.

> **Snowflakes so fleeting,**
> **Created for this instant—**
> **Crystals of God's love.**

With the first buds on the trees, Lemon called a meeting, easy in the cabin, and started it off with this.

29
Gentle, innocent Word betrayed,
Then condemned by Throners cruel,
Carried his cross to the hill of shame,
A king portrayed as a fool.
Naked and nailed, they spurned him still,
"Forgive them, Song," he cried;
Then forsaken, it was finished,
And so in darkness—he died.

An earthquake rocked their feet and hearts;
Poem's veil was torn in two;
Some tombs of Race broke open in droves,
And Word was laid in lieu.
But Word defeated death anew,
And on the third day—he rose.

Then he announced, "This place is much too desolate for my medicine show. There be not enough people around who need my patent nostrums, or trick shooting, or Lotta dancing on tables. Or even sweet Alanna dressed scantily as a wood elf from Muckanagheder Forest. The few people who live here are too busy in the soil of their fields for such mindless diversions. Besides they're Swedish Baptists, ever so strict."

"I thought they were all Lutherans," Étienne said.

"Does it really matter? They're all silly." Lemon stroked his beard. "Swedish immigrants come over here because of religious persecution. The pot calling the kettle black. Unlike wishy-washy Lutherans, they have a strong notion about the Bible being the incessant Word of God. They believe in believer's baptism by dunking three times fully clothed, head-to-toe in cold water. And they want to live holier-than-thou lives as followers of Jesus H. Christ. So why would they pay money for my grog and phony show?"

"Not Jesus H. Christ," Aoife said. "Leave out the H."

Lemon turned toward her. "The H comes from the Christian monogram seen everywhere."

"Well I haven't seen it," said Aoife. "I don't think it's proper use. God's name is so holy we shouldn't even be uttering it, let alone taking it in vain. Exodus 20:7 commands:

You must not misuse the name of the Lord your God. The Lord will not let you go unpunished if you misuse his name.

"How'd you feel if your name was used as a swear word?" Aoife added.

"Aoife, sister, stop being a hypocrite," Bridget said. "The third commandment has a deeper meaning than just swearing. James 1:26 says that if you claim to be a Christian but don't control your mind and body, you're fooling yourself, and your religion is worthless. You bear his name but drag it through sin for the world to see. That's misusing it." She glanced at Faolan.

Lemon ignored her. "Again, the pot calling the kettle black. So pack your things my elven child Alanna and my dear Colleen girl. We leave tomorrow. Lotta stared at him. "And of course you too, Sweetie Pie."

Faolan piped up. "Take Lotta if you must, but not Aoife."

"Why not, what be she to you?" Lemon demanded.

"I'm not going," said Bridget. "We're building another log cabin here, near the Delacroix family."

Lemon pointed his shillelagh at Aoife but she scowled at it, gripped her Bible, and refused to budge. "If my stick won't persuade you then perhaps my six-gun will," he warned.

"Put that away," said Bridget with glassy eyes. "Of course I'm coming. It will be fun."

Aoife hesitated, then looked at the ground. "Well, I'm not staying here without my sister. Are you coming with us Faolan? Looks like we'll be needing to set sail in your prairie schooner again." Her man was a strong ship but easily driven by her every wind and current.

Lemon concluded the morning with this.

30
Hue then spliced some Race to Racer,
If only they'd believe
In Word who lived and died for them,
Their trespass to reprieve.
"Racergraft" received the keys to Love,
Good News indeed for them.
"Go forth, tell all," said Poem Love,
"Through you, my love will stem."
So off they went with Word and care,
To lost world's darkest end.
They learned new speech and tried
To love all that Hue did send—
With many a praise and loud amen,
Countless martyrs died.

That night Étienne asked Bridget for a walk in the woods. She let him for once. He chirped his strident cicada courtship song incessantly to the side of her head. These insects call so loudly they need to be able to unplug their own ears. Not so poor Bridget. So he trilled on. "Ça va? *Ça sent le printemps!* The buds of spring they are here. Seeds are springing up from wet gardens. Green shoots unfold. The meadowlarks are back singing flutelike mating songs. Bullfrogs are bellowing from hot mud. Garter snakes are forming shameless sex balls and giving live birth."

Bridget wrinkled her nose and her ears started turning. "Even if Aoife leaves," he continued, "why don't you to stay with us? We'd build you a nice cabin warm. Don't go with Lemon, that Irish *enchanteur.*

Car il s'élèvera de faux Christs et de faux prophètes; ils feront de grands prodiges et des miracles, au point de séduire, s'il était possible, même les élus."

For false messiahs and false prophets will rise up and perform great signs and wonders so as to deceive, if possible, even God's chosen ones.
Matthew 24:24

"I won't leave my sister," Bridget replied, pushing on his shoulder.

"I'd build you one *fabuleuse* log mansion with a bed fit for queen," he said, stopping to pick her a lone yellow crocus. When she didn't reply, he leaned forward and added something: "Well at least let me to sit with you by the fire of your last night. Before you die to me."

She stared at him. "Fiddlesticks. Sagouin! In all of Wisconsin Territory don't you think there are thousands of fish in the lakes? Some probably even speak French. Besides we are entirely different species, you and me, and it wouldn't be fitting. You stay here. Honour your father. Don't follow me. Put your Frog lips back in your mouth."

Later she told her sister everything and giggled, "I think he wanted to kiss me." Her ears turned crimson and cream, which represent courage and purity.

Fort Snelling

So with the passing of the snow, two of the three wagons headed down the trail west. Faolan drove one with Aoife and Bridget peering out the back. And Lemon the other with Lotta inside on a fluffy bed of goose down. They had left the little Delacroix family behind in their new cabin, but not without a handful of green Connemara marble lucky charms which Lemon promised someday might prove useful. Caitlín considered prayer more effective. Aoife wiped away tears and waved goodbye to her bosom friend. She couldn't help but recall how Saoirse, from the workhouse, wasn't able to come with her either. And the reason. She was chained by a man and his deeds. Caitlín had just secretly told Aoife she was indeed carrying a brother for Aurora.

"Brother? How do you know?" Aoife had asked.

"Lemon told me," Caitlín had said, "but it's a secret until I'm sure and I tell Jean."

At that point her cabin, silhouetted by a big red sun, was disappearing beneath the meadows and

230

only its smoke could be seen circling high. When even that was lost, Aoife climbed into the front of the wagon to be with Faolan. She left Bridget brooding in back and composing a poem for her poor Étienne left behind.

Elvish ice maiden,
My molten heart's now frozen
Fast to our winter.

Scannalan was not at all sad to be leaving Puck behind in Wisconsin Territory where he belonged.

Aoife turned and remarked to her man, "You know, the farther west we go, the fewer people there are going to be. How then will you find your sturdy pioneer girl to marry?"
"God will provide such things," he said.

And God will generously provide all you need.
Then you will always have everything you need and
plenty left over to share with others.
2nd Corinthians 9:8

Aoife shrugged and wondered if this applied to the provision of wives. And the sharing thereof. She wiped some road dust from her eye, and flattened the skirt on her lap.

Further west they finally reached the mighty Mississippi river. But it was quite unimpressive just north of Fort Snelling. There they saw many keelboats—barges that had shallow draughts and keels but no sails—propelled by rowing or punting. A cabin for cargo ran down the middle of each which permitted men to plant long poles in the river bottom and tread along the deck sides to move the boat. As they were waiting for a ferry, they met the captain of one of these on the docks. He was more bear than man, standing six foot three and weighing nigh on two hundred. His name was Miche Phinck but most people called him "the snapping turtle." He was intrigued by Faolan's Irish brogue and boasted to him that he could "out-run, out-shoot, out-hop, out-jump, throw-down, drag out, and lick any man in the country. Out-drink to boot. Especially a Blarney-Paddy."

Bridget marched right up and poked him in his massive belly. "Out-brag, maybe. Betcha yous can't out-gun my Doc Holiday here."

The snapping turtle immediately turned and shot the scalp lock off the head of an Indian standing up on the bluff. Then he had someone nail six aces to a tree at forty paces: three spades and three hearts. Straight away he proceeded to plug one spade square in the middle. "Take the first heart," he said, and Lemon had no trouble doing so. "Now my turn," he said. But as soon as he fired Lemon whipped his pistol around to knock the captain's bullet off course and into the second heart. Lemon's own slug ricocheted to bull's eye the third. The snapping turtle's jaw dropped.

"Doc Holiday's the best shooter outside Ireland," Bridget said. "No brag. Just fact—you Yankee-doodle-noodle." The snapping turtle bristled but knew not to hit a girl. So he bought them all beers and they were very content to let him out-drink them and then out-crawl everyone back to the boats.

About this time Lemon was running low on cash again and lucky for them, a huge sternwheel paddle boat was chug chugging, puffing, and pulling up nearby. As it steam-whistled and lowered its gangplank, Lenna Ó Leannáin marched on-board, hand-in-hand with his miniature show girl and what looked like an adorable green elf—so light on her feet it almost appeared as if she were floating. Soon he had them booked for the evening performance and while they danced for quarters, he recited a poem about love using an especially thick Irish brogue. Few could understand it but the others were enthralled by the waving of his shillelagh.

31
'Racerpaul' a Wordbud Singer,
Sent to the Racergraft,
Through shipwreck, trials and prison cruel,
Proclaiming joy, he laughed.
"Without love, I'm a clanging gong;
Poem's for us, who's against?
At the judgment seat of the Word,
We'll all be recompensed.
We live by faith and not by sight;
Love's power to us consigned.
Whatever you sew, you will reap;
Love is patient, love is kind;
It's through preaching—his Word we find,
Unashamed, gospel we keep."

Later he cleaned up the chips on the poker tables. After six amazingly profitable nights they slipped away in their wagons before the showboat realized they'd been completely bamboozled and befogified.

On their first night away, they camped by a singing brook which inspired Lemon to retrieve his fiddle. After several spirited ditties, this sad ballad spilled out. Bridget sang wet-eyed for her poor, imagined Étienne, "*mon lapin,*" my bunny, left behind.

À la claire fontaine m'en allant promener J'ai trouvé l'eau si belle que je m'y suis baignée.	By the clear fountain, going for a walk I found the water so clear I had to bathe.
Mon petit chou, je t'aime depuis peu, mais jamais je ne t'oublierai.	My little cream puff, I've loved you a short time, but I will never forget you.
Sous les feuilles d'un chêne, je me suis fait sécher. Sur la plus haute branche, un rossignol chantait.	Under the oak's leaves, I lay and dried. On the highest bough, a nightingale sang.
Chante, rossignol, chante, toi qui as le cœur gai. Tu as le cœur à rire… moi je l'ai à pleurer.	Sing, nightingale, sing, you of the joyous heart. Your heart is to laugh, mine is to cry.
J'ai perdu mon ami sans l'avoir mérité, Pour un bouton de rose que je lui refusai. Je voudrais que la rose fût encore au rosier,	I lost my friend, which I didn't deserve, For a rosebud I kept from him. I wish the rose still on the bush,

| Et que mon doux ami | And my sweet friend |
| fût encore à m'aimer. | still loving me. |

As she laid her head on the pillow, her eyes closed and her cheeks paled. Her breathing hushed. One of her hands felt limp. "Perchance, do elves live forever?" she wondered. "I grow weary of being a fifth wheel on this wagon. My sorrow is a sea without a shore."

In the morning, a tall Ojibwe Indian approached them. "*Boozhoo*," he said, grunting their traditional greeting. Underneath an army blanket, used as a parka, he was wearing a tanned deerskin breechcloth tucked into a decorated belt. Also leggings, a separate one for each leg and moccasins, one for each foot. Bridget thought his cloth must be simply a washrag hung from the belt and he would be naked underneath. There is nothing bolder than a curious elf so she marched right up to him and lifted a corner. She found that the cloth wound over the belt, under him, and then over the belt again in back. So all she saw was the rest of his loincloth, looking like underwear. The Indian bristled but grinned and knew not to hit a girl.

He told Lemon they could purchase supplies downriver at Fort Snelling where the Mississippi joins the Minnesota River. "The Mississippi flows all the way to New Orleans," he said.

"How do you know that?" asked Bridget.

"Tell us about this Fort Smelling," Lemon said. "It was built in 1819 to control British traders in the Iowa Territory," he told Lemon in his native language, *Anishinaabemowin*, "and make a barrier between the hated Dakota Sioux and us Ojibwe. We are constantly fighting and hundreds of scalps are hanging in our tipis. But a cross hangs in mine."

Lemon translated for Bridget. "Are you a Christian?" she asked. "Then why are you wearing a turkey feather?"

"Why are you in elvish hair-dress?" he responded. "And it's eagle, not turkey." Turning to Lemon, he continued. "Twenty years ago the fort was commanded by Lieutenant Colonel Zachary Taylor. He was the one whose daughter eloped with the son of Lieutenant Jefferson Davis—to be married in the blockhouse. Later as president, Taylor ordered the removal of all Indians to Kansas. Christian missionaries protested and after Taylor's death his successor, Millard Fillmore rescinded the order. These missionaries adopted and educated me. They taught our warriors to give up man's work, hunting, for woman's work, farming, but with European style, horse drawn plows. I wear this Eagle feather because I'm still proud to be an Ojibwe. Yet, I love my saviour Jesus Christ even more. He doesn't require us to become White Men."

Lenna Ó Leannáin bought supplies at Fort Snelling and the soldiers there enjoyed several performances by the *Doc Holliday's Winnebago Medicine Show* troupe. Lotta was a particular hit prancing about on the long mess tables. Her heels clicked excitingly on the pine planks as her curls danced to Lemon's fiddle tunes. On purpose, she

slipped and plunged into a burly sergeant's arms. The money she earned from such tumbles paid for their supplies and then some. And of course there was his poetry.

32
"Know the wages of sin is death,
But rejoice in Song always,
For his free gift is eternal life,
Secure in all ways, all days.
Do not be yoked with scoffers vile,
Or lust about in shame,
For you are a new creation,
Thus live! And to die is gain.
So put off anger, wrath, malice, filth;
Honour your father and mother.
Poem cannot be mocked;
Love every man a brother,
And worship Poem like no other.
Faith must not be rocked."

Reverend Ezekiel Filbert Bear, D.D., the fort chaplain soon came around to ascertain if this Doc Holliday was really a wizard or heretic as was being widely reported. He also wanted to find out if the shows were above boards and especially if the "miracle elixirs" were genuine. The surgeon, Doctor Emerson referred to them as "sinister turpentine" after his slave Dred Scott had purchased a bottle.

"I didn't know there were slaves this far north," Aoife remarked to Lemon.

"He's originally from the South," Lemon said, "and therefore remains a slave anywhere he is taken."

"Not in Ireland, he wouldn't be," she said. "I'm a slave for Jesus Christ, you know."

Even though I am a free man with no master, I have become a slave to all people to bring many to Christ.
1st Corinthians 9:19

"Slowly, I'm saving you from that, my dear Colleen." Lemon said. "Freedom is choosing for yourself and doing what is right in your own eyes." Bridget walked up, took his hand, and snuggled into his cape.

Reverend Bear then asked about their living arrangements. He soon found out that none of them were related to each other, yet living in only two small wagons.

Bridget piped up, "Oh, that's okay. Lotta's like Lemon's daughter and I think of Aoife as a sister. Faolan's sweet on her but I won't let him anysnugglewhere near her. I said 'put a ring on it first,' I did."

"*Honi soit qui mal y pense,*" Lemon said, "May he be shamed who thinks evil of it."

Reverend Bear replied immediately. "There's such a thing as avoiding the appearance of evil.

Stay away from every kind of evil.
1st Thessalonians 5:22

"That's important in this day and age. Especially in front of these soldiers and recent Indian converts." He turned to Aoife. "Please let me marry you as soon as possible." Faolan came up and took her hand.

Lemon interjected again, waving his finger. "I am her saviour guardian and I would not give my consent to any such human ritual."

"Sir, you have no legal standing in this matter," said the chaplain. "I will be available as early as tomorrow morning to make matters right and also to look into your relationship with the little curly-haired dancing girl." He bounded off. Lemon followed.

Aoife looked at Faolan.

May we meet in heaven's peace;
May his heat in hell increase.

Through the Wagon Wheel

That night she found him under his wagon fixing a wheel. She addressed his feet. "There's such a thing as avoiding the appearance of evil. It's important in this day and age. Please let me marry you as soon as possible. Let me be your sturdy pioneer girl and I'll give you love and lovely children to your lonely heart's content."

There was the sound of grunting and squirming under the wagon. Then a greasy fist appeared from between the spokes. Slowly it opened to reveal one of Bridget's diamond rings rescued from her treasure months ago. "She told me 'to put a ring on it,' she did."

"You just carry that around in your pocket all the time?" the girl snapped. It was too big for her finger, to massive for her tastes, and not delivered on one knee as dreamed but she grasped it anyway. "Son of a gun," she said, "I reckon it's fitting we get engaged through a wagon wheel, but can we please settle down soon in a small cottage on gentle hills by a trout stream—with a living room, kitchen, and the big brass bed? And two goose down pillows in lace covers?"

"There're so many Canadian Geese around," Faolan said, "pillow ready. I don't see no problems with any of that." When he rolled out from under the wagon his face looked like Scannalan's. But it was beautiful to her.

Lemon was against the marriage and wanted to take Aoife further west the very next day. But Faolan wanted to buy land near the fort for protection. So the commandant sent them downstream a bit to a place across the river called *L'Œil du Cochon,* The Pig's Eye. "They'll tell you where you can settle," he said.

Aoife confronted Lemon there in the rustic tavern. "Thanks for the delicious meal, but I can no longer be your slave. You move in me unnaturally but Faolan is the stronger force of human love." Lemon reached for his shillelagh. "No," Aoife grabbed it first, "the marriage bond will soon overwhelm all other powers. Christ has become my only rod and staff. With it, I'll break your throne."

The next evening a missionary to the Dakota Sioux Indians married Aoife O'Day and Faolan Rogan right there in the saloon. He had lost his Preacher's Handbook so it was a most simple affair. Nobody dressed up—or messed up while reading from an old Irish book they found on a shelf in the bar. Even a resigned Lenna Ó Leannáin agreed to participate.

A washed up Faolan began with his vows. Despite his many muscles, his hands shook and his knees wobbled.

Faolan's vow:
"I pledge my love to you, and everything that I own. I promise you the first bite of my meat and the first sip from by cup. I pledge that your name will always be the name I cry aloud in the dead of night. I promise to honour you above all others. Our love is never-ending, and we will remain, forevermore, partners in our marriage. This is my wedding vow to you. **Tugaim mo chroí duit go deo** *- I give my heart to you forever."*

Aoife stood regal and erect. In her steady hand she carried her sharkskin Bible, purchased by 63 lives lost at sea, and one special person on the cross—lovingly handcrafted by her husband-to-be, and 40 writers, several translators—and one author.

Aoife's vow:
"By the power that Christ brought from heaven, mayst thou love me. As the sun follows its course, mayst thou follow me. As light to the eye, as bread to the hungry, as joy to the heart, May thy presence be with me, oh one that I love, `til death comes to part us asunder. You are the kernel of my heart, you are the face of my sun, you are the harp of my music, you are the crown of my company. **Tá mo chroí istigh ionat -** *My heart is within you."*

There was an awkward pause so Bridget peeked from behind Lemon's cloak to address Aoife directly.

Bridget's Blessing:
M'anam cara, our bond has been earned, not inherited.

242

Effey, you are the star of each night,
You are the brightness of every morning,
No evil shall befall you, on hill nor bank,
In field or valley, on mountain nor in glen.
Neither above, nor below, neither in sea,
Nor on shore, in skies above,
Nor in the depths.
You are the kernel of my heart,
You are the face of my sun,
You are the harp of my music,
You are the crown of my company.

Then she poked the old man behind her. "Say something nice," she muttered.

Lemon's blessing:
"You cannon possess each other for you are individuals. But while you both wish it, give to each other that which is yours to give. You cannon command each other, for you are free people. But shall serve each other in those ways you require and the honeycomb will taste sweeter coming from each other's hands. Be shields for each other. Be as sun to a flower and seed to a wet garden. Reserve your lips for loving, never slander. When you quarrel do so in private and tell no strangers your grievances. Honour each other as the stars of each night, and the brightness of every morning in a marriage of equals as long as you both shall love."

Faolan and Aoife turned uneasily into each other and joined hands.

The couple's vow together:
"We swear by peace and love as one to stand, heart to heart and hand to hand, in Christ till death

do us part. Mark, O Holy Spirit, and hear us now,
confirming this our Sacred Vow."

There was another silence so the missionary
raised his hands and pronounced:

The missionary's blessing:
May God be with you and bless you;
May you see your children's children.
May you be poor in misfortune,
Rich in blessings,
May you know nothing but happiness
From this day forward.

May the road rise to meet you
May the wind be always at your back
May the warm rays of sun fall upon your home
The rains fall soft upon your fields.
May God hold you in the palm of his hand.

May green be the grass you walk on,
May blue be the skies above you,
May pure be the joys that surround you,
May true be the hearts that love you.

After this he led in an old hymn:

The heav'ns declare Thy glory, Lord,
In every star Thy wisdom shines
But when our eyes behold Thy Word,
We read Thy Name in fairer lines.

The rolling sun, the changing light,
And nights and days, Thy power confess
But the blest volume Thou hast writ

Reveals Thy justice and Thy grace.

Sun, moon, and stars convey Thy praise
Round the whole earth, and never stand:
So when Thy truth begun its race,
It touched and glanced on every land.

Nor shall Thy spreading Gospel rest
Till through the world Thy truth has run,
Till Christ has all the nations blest
That see the light or feel the sun.

Great Sun of Righteousness, arise,
Bless the dark world with heav'nly light;
Thy Gospel makes the simple wise,
Thy laws are pure, Thy judgments right.

Thy noblest wonders here we view
In souls renewed and sins forgiv'n;
Lord, cleanse my sins, my soul renew,
And make Thy Word my guide to Heaven.

Then abruptly, "I now pronounce you husband and wife. *From the beginning of the creation God made them male and female. For this cause shall a man leave his father and mother, and cleave to his wife; And they twain shall be one flesh: so then they are no more twain, but one flesh. What therefore God hath joined together, let not man put asunder.*" Mark 10:6-9 KJV.

The missionary concluded with this: "Soon Christ will be coming back to defeat Satan and claim us as his own bride, the church. This indeed, is the whole story of the Bible."

Kill the dragon and get the girl!

After the pronouncement the Ojibwe Indian departed. "*Minnow a yog,*" he called, "all of you be well, and live in God's blessings Mr and Mrs Rogan." Some Irish coffee followed but the couple had already retreated to their honeymoon wagon to begin their new life together—planting seeds in fertile wet fields. Aoife avoided her husband's eyes but whispered a poem into his ear.

> I've got a secret pocket, I wear it just for me.
> It's not a patch or locket,
> That anyone can see.
> It has my hidden doubts and fears,
> Safely tucked away—
> Protects me from my shames and tears,
> And that is where they'll stay.
> Even when we're naked pressed,
> My pocket is still there.
> And I confess I never guessed,
> You had one too, my honey bear.
> Now as our love is digging deep,
> And doubts and fears are scattered,
> The secret pocket things we keep—
> Never really mattered.

Faolan replied—she'd been teaching him how to be a poet.

> You crash on my rocks and lap at my sand,
> Making waves on the beach, our rhythmic shore,
> The tides of our hearts, nature's demand;
> Whatever seems less, will soon become more.

Bridget, abandoned, wandered about outside— alone well into the night. When it began to rain she snuck into the back of Lemon's wagon and cuddled up next to Lotta at his feet. "It's only rain on my face," she whispered. But the girl wiped it away with a finger and found it salty to taste. "Does he do anything to you at night?" Bridget asked.

"Oh yes," Lotta said. "He snores. Here's some cotton for your ears."

Entering the medicine wagon in the dark, Bridget had fumbled for the latch and accidently released a rattlesnake to the ground. Calmly she had severed its head with a shovel and slung the rest over into the bushes. Later, on a trip to the outhouse she noticed the head was still there so she stooped to pick it up. As she tossed it away a needle-like fang stung her finger. She thought little of it until a few days later when it started to discolour. "Oh, it's nothing," she told Lotta.

With Aoife lost to him, Lemon wanted to head west with his Bridget and Lotta before the army chaplain came snooping around again. The problem was that every remedy he tried on Bridget's baby finger failed. Slowly the discoloration was spreading to the rest of her hand. She was becoming listless and unfit for travel. She'd just sit for days on the edge of the wagon and write page after page with her good hand in a book of bound sheets she'd bought in Boston. She even put some drawings in it. But she refused meals and all company except Scannalan who served as a nice warm pillow for her bad arm.

"I hate God," she said over and over to herself. "Either he can't heal me or he won't. Both are equally bad. How much pain must I bear before he's satisfied? With my black arm and what's left of my tortured mind I curse him. How dead must I be before I can find new life? I helped others to die but now I'm powerless to help myself."

Then she remembered Romans 8:38-39 from Aoife's Bible.

And I am convinced that nothing can ever separate us from God's love. Neither death nor life, neither angels nor demons, neither our fears for today nor our worries about tomorrow—not even the powers of hell can separate us from God's love. No power in the sky above or in the earth below— indeed, nothing in all creation will ever be able to separate us from the love of God that is revealed in Christ Jesus our Lord.

Who lives for Jesus?
And life or death's always gain?
But can't shake snakes off.

Yes, God seemed distant, lost to her. "No, this can't be happening to me." It was increasingly hard to write even with her good hand. "I'm the main character in this book," she said, "the sweet sprite everyone adores. Étienne loved me as a woman. Aoife as a sister even if she left me for Caitlín, then Faolan. Lemon loves me for the impish elf I am. So I cannot die. How can I be writing me out of my own book? I'll go back East, build a house on my land, and marry a rich Boston Brahmin. If I write that elves live forever, will that make it true? It's my book; I can make it so." But all she wanted to do was sleep.

That night she penned the last word and stole over to Faolan's wagon. She had trouble getting up into it. They were over in the tavern selfishly laughing with the crowd. Gently she placed the book on the shelf next to Aoife's Bible and headed back in the blackness. But soon she was overcome with sleep and laid down in the soft grass. Somehow a prayer came into her mind.

I have been a voyager across life's oceans; Safe in heaven's ark, passing through a troubled world into the harbour of eternal rest. I amn't afraid to look the king of terrors in the face, for I know I shall be drawn, not driven, out of the world. Until then let me continually glow and burn out for thee, and when the last great change shall come let me awake in thy likeness, leaving behind me an example that will glorify thee, while my spirit rejoices in heaven, and my memory is blessed upon earth, with those who follow me praising thee for my life.

"But nobody really praises me," she said out loud as if arguing with herself, "not even God. Especially not God. Please Mommy, I'm holding on. Help me, Spirit of Grace, get up from this ground. It's cold. It's so cold. I can't by myself."

They buried Bridget Galadriel Alatáriel three miles southwest of Fort Snelling. It was in a secluded, wooded area and without ceremony because Lemon wanted to avoid the clergy. He took back the fancy clothes and dressed her in her original burlap sack. He'd kept it among his things all this time. Still tucked in the pocket was a lucky charm, not of much use to her now. There was no shroud, no headstone.

"But there will be nothing to remember her by," Lotta said. "I trust I'll be remembered better than this."

Who can quench the sun,
Forget a girl, hide the moon,
Or hold back the stars?

"Well, just think of the coordinates here," Lemon said. "44° 52′ 11″ N, 93° 12′ 51″ W. Those numbers will bring back the fond memories of our dear elf Alanna, which means my child who will never die. She was my special Iníon."

Aoife spoke over the tiny body:

Her identity—
Was not in herself achieved,
But in Christ received.

"Farewell Biddy, my dear sister."

God spoke creation;
He wrote His holy scriptures—
But SINGS over you.
                              Zephaniah 3:17

250

Lemon ended with this.

33
In seven cycles of seven,
Poem, end times arrayed;
"I am alpha and Omega,"
Seven churches portrayed.
Worthy is the Lion, the Lamb,
To break scroll's seven seals;
At the seventh trumpet's triumph.
He returns! Every church bell peals.
As Gracie gives birth to the Word,
Glare longs to be fed;
Seven bowls of wrath poured out upon Race
Glare and Babylon war dead,
Word to judge from throne of dread,
Heaven and earth to replace.

The grave would be forever forgotten but soon they found Bridget's book titled Aoife's Bible, penned in her own hand, and placed snuggly next to Aoife's Bible. Aoife whispered these last words to her.

Again and again,
To my Bible you said no—
But in death amen?

Chapter 9

Epilogue

On July 4th, 1876 the Museum of Fine Arts opened at 138 St. James Avenue, Boston. The reclaimed land had been abandoned by one Bridget O'Day and ceded to the Commonwealth of Massachusetts.

Lenna Ó Leannáin continued on west with Lotta and she made quite a name for herself in the saloons. The bottom of their wagon became filled with so many coins and nuggets they had trouble crossing rivers. Scannalan was posted day and night as a guard but it was actually Lemon's famous six-guns which deterred any funny stuff. Due to their notoriety, Lotta's mother, Maryann Crabtree finally caught up with her in Tombstone, Arizona and whisked her off to the California gold rush, well in time to make another fortune. Later in life, Lotta bought a hotel back in Boston, which had been converted from an art museum. Books have been written about her. Lemon did OK as well. He survived a famous gunfight in a horse corral and much later died of natural causes in his bed in Glenwood Springs, Colorado. His last words were about God.

34
Worthy One had rescued dead Race,
From Folly, Scowl and Glare;
And faced the thunder music Song,
Saving many, but not me there—
As he was mocked, the nails were mine,
I loved myself anew,
And pandered earthly pleasures fine,
To man and girl and you.
Now at the end, I've but my guns,
To shoot my own way free.
My house of cards, with tinsel walls,
Are naught of worth to me
And all my targets paper be,
In death, I spurn Love's calls.

So all of Lemon's Irish luck and prosperity was
in fact the trial which kept him from the Lord. His
obituary in the local newspaper claimed "his *Coca-
Cola* and *Lemon-up,* marketed as *Seven-up,* made
him rich but the concoctions were irresponsible for
more deaths than his six-guns." His tombstone
contained only one word:

<Aiwendil>

And buried with him were many ancient things
perhaps best forgotten for all time. Except one. The
moment of his last breath, an epic Poem about her
Saviour popped into Aoife's head.

Caitlín and Father Doctor Jean Marie Delacroix
remained in Wisconsin all their days, treating the
sick and raising Aurora with many other children,
several of whom were orphans and Indians.

Étienne Delacroix found another pretty elf to marry but was killed on his birthday five years later on September 17, 1862 in the Battle of Antietam. It was the costliest single day of fighting in American history with more than 22,000 casualties. The standoff emboldened Abraham Lincoln to emancipate the slaves, but most, like Dred Scott, never became truly free at all. Étienne's wife and father didn't get word of his death for several years and they never recovered the body. Yet he was truly free indeed.

Aoife and Faolan Rogan stayed in Minnesota and planted vegetables, wheat, hay, and raised cattle. She wrote poetry. In addition they peopled much of the eastern part of that state. Their descendants finally put Aoife's Bible into a museum. Its pages were well-worn but the cover remained as sturdy as the day it was fished out of the sea. Next to it, they placed the journal, Aoife's Bible, dusty, dog-eared, and yellowing with age. On the last page the curator discovered some tiny, hidden letters near the binding—fresh ink in spidery elvish runes.

*Le grá go **deo*** - With love **forever**

Contents

Characters

Aoife (EE-fa) – an orphan, 7
Bridget – a young female, 11
Caitlín – (KAHT-leen) Shaughnessy – a Catholic girl, 72
Einin (EH-neen) – a girl saved in the workhouse, 49
Étienne (eh-TsYEN) – Jean's son, 145
Faolan (FWAIL-awn) Rogan – a seaman, 76
Jean Marie Delacroix (žawn ma REE DEL a kwa) – a Doctor
    and Priest, 13
Lenna Ó Leannáin (Lemon) – a wizard, 21
Muirín (MIR-een) – a baby aborted at sea, 107
Saoirse (SAIR-sha) – a pagan girl from the workhouse, 42

Illustrations

Glossary for *Poem Love*

Feed=Plants

Gigantors=Giants

Glare=Satan

Glares=Fallen Angels

Glowers=Angels

Grace=Woman, Eve

Gracie=Mary

Hue=The Holy Spirit

Pets=Animals

Pneuma=Spirit

Poem Love=God

Poets=prophets

Psychē=Soul

Race=Man, Mankind

Racer=Israel

Racergraft=Church

Robeys=Judges, Priests

Scowls=Demons

Singers=Missionaries

Sōma=Body

Song=God the Father

Tabletations=The Law

Throner=King

Thronie=Queen

Wild=Wilderness

Word=Christ

Wordbud=Apostle

Worthy One=Christ

Scriptures

Index & Glossary

262

www.ingramcontent.com/pod-product-compliance
Lightning Source LLC
Chambersburg PA
CBHW030400020726
47493CB00003B/894